P9-EJY-831

— WESLEY ELLIS —

LONE STAR

AND THE
OKLAHOMA AMBUSH

JOVE BOOKS, NEW YORK

LONE STAR AND THE OKLAHOMA AMBUSH

A Jove Book / published by arrangement with
the author

PRINTING HISTORY
Jove edition / March 1991

ISBN: 0-515-10527-9

Jove Books are published by The Berkley Publishing Group,
200 Madison Avenue, New York, New York 10016.
The name "JOVE" and the "J" logo
are trademarks belonging to Jove Publications, Inc.

PRINTED IN THE UNITED STATES OF AMERICA

10 9 8 7 6 5 4 3 2 1

Chapter 1

Graham Greenleaf leaned back against the settee's plush cushions and gazed into Esmeralda Harcourt's watery gray eyes. The heavy scent of lavender clogged the air in the living room, making relaxed breathing almost impossible. He crossed his long, slender legs and bounced a shiny boot on a knee as if enjoying himself immensely. Casually, he shook his head, a wry smile tugging at the corners of his mouth, and kept total eye contact at all times.

"I don't believe it!" he said, putting up a hand before the old woman could reply. "Now, please don't misunderstand me—I would never think of calling you a prevaricator, Mrs. Harcourt—but truth be told, there's no way on God's green earth I'm gonna believe you are a day over sixty."

"But—"

He smiled and nibbled on a square of fresh gingerbread, washing it down with strong, rapidly cooling tea. "I'm sorry," he said as he wiped the reddish tips of his deep brown mustache with the corner of a lace napkin, "but you're far too young and vibrant to be anywheres near sixty."

The seventy-three-year-old grandmother of two flushed as she must have only in decades past, her translucent cheeks coloring with the heat of excitement. As she brushed aside a strand of white hair from her wrinkled forehead, she felt the sudden radiance of her flesh. She smoothed out the skirt of her best

1

silk frock, the silver gray one she always wore to show off the color of her eyes.

"I assure you, Mr. Greenleaf, I am almost old enough to be your mother." She smiled demurely, looking at him from under lowered lids. She giggled and sipped her tea. "Well, at least, your older sister."

"Ah, Mrs. Harcourt," he said, hooking a thumb in the vest of his neat broadcloth suit, "to have a sister as lovely as you would be illegal. Truth be told, ma'am, I could never bear to have you for a sister of mine. Why, it would break my heart." He placed the delicate cup and saucer on the table next to him, his intense hazel eyes never leaving hers. "In fact, I'm not even sure I want to go on with this."

"Oh?"

His smile almost turned to a leer, but he caught himself in time and coughed, the back of his hand covering his mouth, as he cleared his throat in a gentlemanly manner. He hoped the old woman would note the perfection of his smooth, blemish-free palm, unmarked by the coarseness of work-related calluses.

Esmeralda Harcourt dropped her gaze and reached for the lace fan she kept on the table beside her. Shining wisps of white hair fluttered in the breeze of her flustered attempt to cool her ignited passions. She pulled a delicate handkerchief from her sleeve and daubed her forehead and upper lip. It became apparent that the gentleman's charms had made an impression, and she tried to keep herself from perspiring, since ladies never glowed in public.

Graham Greenleaf, in an overt gesture of good manners, shifted his gaze to the pictures around the room—no male over forty in any of them, he noted. A portrait above the fireplace mantel and a tintype in a prominent place on the large table by the old lady's arm gave him a clue. The painting—a young bride and groom in full wedding attire—proclaimed the happiness of the day, and the bride's resemblance to Esmeralda Harcourt was more than fleeting. The tintype of the same couple probably twenty-five years later could only have been Esmeralda and her Harold.

There were no pictures of the groom past the age of forty or so. From this, Graham Greenleaf surmised that it had been many years since someone had kept company with this aged widow. He could tell she was not accustomed to being paid compliments, and flattery—even the most sincere he could muster—obviously rattled and unsettled her. Thirty years, Greenleaf estimated, she'd been widowed. He checked each picture and face again before speaking.

"Are you sure you have no one to advise you on this, Mrs. Harcourt?" he asked, appearing appropriately concerned. "I would never want it said that Graham Greenleaf or the Henerow Corporation took advantage of you, my dear." He reached for another large piece of gingerbread and smiled appreciatively as his hostess jumped up to pour him more tea.

"Oh, my, no," she said, dumping a heaping spoonful of brownish sugar into the cup of hot liquid. "My Harold's been gone for well over thirty-three years now, God rest and keep his blessed soul." She gazed at the marriage portrait above the mantel and sighed deeply.

Greenleaf grinned inwardly as his brows knit in a sympathetic frown. He'd only been off by three years—pretty good, but no blue ribbon. Inwardly, he admonished himself for missing by so much. He should have been able to peg her down to the month—after all, sizing people up was his business, his stock in trade.

"Of course," she continued, warming to his welcome empathy, "there's my late son's children—Hubert, Jr., and Halleybelle." She sipped her tea quietly and glanced off toward the thick hand-hewn mantel and several pictures in silver frames. "My Hubert and his Arabella passed on in an accident on the way home from church services several years ago." Her face darkened with the pain of an unbidden memory. "Flash flood," she said crisply, letting Graham Greenleaf know the subject was concluded.

"I'm so sorry. I didn't mean to pry." He looked properly chagrined as he took a long drink of tepid tea and stared at the portraits. "It is most difficult to picture you as a grandmother, but by now your grandchildren must be old enough to advise you?"

Her cheeks dimpled as she smiled. "Oh, my goodness, no. They're just babies."

3

Greenleaf nodded, laughing lightly at her amusement. From what he'd heard from her neighbors and friends, Esmeralda Harcourt's grandchildren were in their twenties and quite competent adults. Fortunate for him that she still saw them as mindless tots to be ignored where business was concerned. She would have been much more difficult to fleece had she put any store in what her grandson had to say, but with her near-senile attitude, she would be easy pickins—and the grandson would be almost powerless to stop him.

"I understand," he said. "Well, obviously, if you've been alone for so many years, you must have a good sense for business or you would never have survived." He watched the crinkles of her cheeks push her eyes nearly shut as the old woman beamed her approval. He laughed, a well-mannered guffaw, and continued as if he had at first censored himself and then decided to share his thought with her. "Of course, Mrs. Harcourt—dare I call you Esmeralda?—truth be told, I have always held to the belief that women—such fragile and lovely creatures—are innately more clever than the world would ever give credit." He winked at her. "I bet you are a little dickens with figures, aren't you?"

"How odd you should mention that." The old woman's smile broadened. "Why, my Harold always told me that I should have been born a man, what with the way I took to numbers and all." She looked up, trying hard to remember. "Now, what was it he used to say . . . ? Oh, yes, my Harold always said I had a right good head for business and"—she giggled—"a nose for numbers."

The old woman's self-effacing titter made Greenleaf grit his back teeth, but with his jaw clenched tightly, he smiled and nodded again. "You see?" He shook a long, well-kempt finger at her. "I knew it! I could tell. No wonder you read the stock certificate so closely. You were merely toying with me, weren't you? You already knew their worth." He grinned and waggled his finger at her. "Naughty girl!" he teased.

"Oh, Mr. Greenleaf, you've found me out." Her girlish giggle betrayed her extreme pleasure at being taunted. "Actually, I hoped you would reconsider and sell me more of the Henerow stock. I've 'slept on it,' as you advised, and I feel it's too good a buy to pass up. I'm prepared to buy much more than your original suggestion. I do hope I'm not too late to make a much larger purchase." She picked up the gilt-edged parchment stock share from the table beside her and fingered it. "I wouldn't want to appear greedy, but would ten times the amount I originally agreed to buy be all right?" Her voice grew anxious. "I'd pay in cash, of course." Her little gray eyes clouded. "Please tell me I'm not too late, Mr. Greenleaf."

Stunned, Graham Greenleaf sipped the residue of tea while his racing brain tried to catch up with this astonishing turn of events. Usually his victims tried to buy less of the worthless stock than he suggested, or perhaps a few shares more for good measure, but no one had ever insisted on purchasing ten times as much as already agreed upon. Could this be a trap? Was she working with the sheriff or the state police?

Above all else, professional swindlers must remain calm and play out the hand as dealt. He had been in the business too many years to be caught completely off guard by some old widder woman, but there was always a first time for the confidence man to be conned.

"I don't know," he said casually, rubbing his leather boot and slowly changing knees. "I wouldn't want you to overstretch yourself financially. I realize you have an exceptionally good mind for figures, but ten times as many shares?"

"Please, Mr. Greenleaf, don't make me plead. I'll understand if you haven't the shares to sell. But, you see, it's an investment for my grandchildren's future." She gazed lovingly at the silver-framed pictures. "All I have to leave them is this ranch and a few holdings in town. I want to assure their financial security, and Henerow Oil is just the ticket."

Graham Greenleaf gulped and waited—there had to be a catch somewhere.

The old woman put aside her cup and saucer and perched herself on the edge of her seat. "My Harold always said that Oklahoma Territory is oil country—he could smell it, he said. But if there's no oil under his land here, then at least I can buy stock in a promising oil venture and provide for Hubert, Jr., and Halleybelle."

Greenleaf struggled to keep his composure but began to relax

5

just a little as the elderly widow prattled on in apparent sincerity.

"I've been here in Harcourtville for as long as I can recollect—long before this region was named as Indian territory—and my Harold had always hoped he'd strike it rich in this wilderness—gold, silver, oil. Instead, he just built himself a town and a ranch and raised cattle along the Cimarron River."

Just built a town? the confidence man thought to himself. A slight nod of Greenleaf's head was enough to keep the woman going.

"It would have broken his heart"—her voice faltered as her eyes filled with tears she refused to shed—"if he had lived to see Texas, Colorado, and Kansas make statehood, and his little patch of ground left out in the cold like some kinda stepchild!"

The slender man clucked his tongue in commiseration, his brows peaking. Involuntarily, he removed the large Waltham pocket watch from his vest and twirled it on its heavy gold chain.

She shook herself and smiled. "But that's another story. Right now, I got a chance here—thanks to you, Mr. Greenleaf—to make my Harold's dream come true." She reached across the table and placed her soft hand on his. "It would make me very happy"—her voice caught as she pleaded, and she struggled to get the words out—"if you would sell me enough stock to ensure my darlings' future."

Greenleaf gulped the last of the tea and wiped his mustache again. Chuckling warmly, he took her hand in both of his. "Why, truth be told, my dear Esmeralda, I could never say no to anyone as lovely and charming as you."

★
Chapter 2

Jessica Starbuck tossed the telegram back to Ki, her large cat-green eyes reading the words once again as the paper lay on the huge butcher's block kitchen table between them. This was not the way to start the day, she reflected, but she felt pleased that her friends had thought to summon her. The wire's contents seemed to flicker as the flame from the oil lamp danced, its light shining brightly on the printed letters. Although it was morning, the cavernous kitchen's expanse needed additional light all day long.

The word *urgent* appeared four times in the telegram's five short sentences, underscoring the sender's plea and the importance of the message:

JESSICA STARBUCK
CIRCLE STAR RANCH, TEXAS

JESSIE: GRANDMA HARCOURT DEAD. STOP. URGENT YOU COME. STOP. PLEASE HELP US. STOP. MUST SEE YOU URGENTLY. STOP. WE NEED YOUR HELP URGENTLY. STOP.
 WITH UTMOST URGENCY, HALLEYBELLE HARCOURT

Ki nodded as he reread the short message and asked, "Isn't this the Halleybelle Harcourt you correspond with? I remember you mentioning something about her just last week, or am I imagining things?"

"No, you're not," Jessie said as she shook her head, her lavish honey-blond tresses tumbling about her shoulders. She reached off to the side and plucked a large bundle of folded pages from her standing desk. "Just last Monday-week I received a letter from Halleybelle." Jessie glanced down at the thick sheaf covered with tiny script and handed the letters to Ki.

He bounced the heavy sheaf in his hand before putting the pages on the table between them.

Jessie continued, "We've been writing to each other for years. Remember, I told you how her father and my father were such old friends? In fact, I wouldn't be surprised if you had met Hubert Halley Harcourt in San Francisco back when you first joined Father."

Ki strained his memory but came up empty as Marguerita cleared the kitchen table of breakfast dishes.

Jessie offered, "Hubert Harcourt's father was Harold Halley Harcourt, the tycoon who built Harcourtville in what's now Oklahoma Territory. Hubert, the son, traveled west, where he met my father, then returned to take care of his mother when his father died early."

Ki snapped his fingers. "Of course, I remember now. That tall fellow with the bright red hair and silver blue eyes had a way with him. Temper so short, your father gave him a wide berth when those blue eyes flashed." Ki smiled warmly as he allowed a rush of memories to overtake him. "So he got married and had a daughter, huh?"

"And a son—Hubert, Jr.—who's older than Halleybelle, by a few years." Jessie picked up the telegram and the letter, her eyes trying to wring additional information from the more recent message. "How long will it take you to secure everything here? Their ranch is almost directly north of here, just on the Cimarron, somewhere between Texas and Colorado. We could take the next train to Oklahoma City and a coach from there to Harcourtville, or we could travel light and ride straight there."

Ki pulled himself out of the comfortable padded kitchen chair and headed for the door, saying, "I'll saddle up our mounts while you pack. And I'll tell Tom to pass the word that we're off. The Circle Star's in good hands with him and his men."

In Spanish, Jessie told the plump housekeeper of their plans. Marguerita, accustomed to her señorita's sudden departures, merely nodded, passed a soapy cloth over the heavy pottery platters and poured hot water from the steaming kettle to rinse them.

Even before Ki left the room, Jessie slipped off the red kimono he had given her for her last birthday. Barefooted and bare, she ran down the long corridor to her bedroom. She jumped into a pair of well-worn jeans and pulled on a soft light-green blouse and a leather riding vest. She sat only long enough to tug on her most comfortable boots, then strapped on her gunbelt and checked the bullets in her .45 Colt revolver. Satisfied, she rolled up a change of clothes and a few pieces of feminine clothing she might need in Harcourtville and trotted out to the stables.

Ki and the foreman, Tom Hollander, stood with both horses ready as Jessie mounted quickly. She tightened the string under her chin to hold her Spanish-style flat-crown hat in place and waited for Tom to tie her bedroll and extra clothes behind her. She shifted impatiently in the saddle until the rangy foreman patted the palomino's rump and stood off to the side.

"Tom, please send a telegram to Halleybelle Harcourt—there's a wire from her on the kitchen table with her address on it—telling her we're on our way." She smiled, not waiting for his response, and galloped off with Ki just one step behind her.

"Yes, ma'am," Tom called as the sorrel gelding and the palomino mare and their riders thundered off. "Things sure happen fast around here," he muttered to himself as he ambled off to the kitchen. The residual aroma of fried bacon and eggs caused his stomach to growl, even though he had already had a full breakfast less than an hour ago. "Hey, Marguerita, any more bacon?" he asked, pointing to the huge skillet and rubbing his belly, wishing he could remember the Spanish word for bacon.

Marguerita wagged a finger at him menacingly, then laughed. *"Sí, tocino,"* she said, reaching for the large slab

9

of fatty salt pork. Deftly, she sliced off several thick pieces of bacon and placed them into the massive black cast-iron skillet.

As he waited for a second breakfast, Tom Hollander scratched the slight overhang of his belly and casually glanced down at the telegram, then read it through. A sudden frown crinkled his dark complexion, and he waved at the housekeeper and the frying bacon. "No, Marguerita, *gracias*, not now!"

Baffled by his change of mind, Marguerita shared some of her thoughts on the subject with the world, yelling in her native tongue for everyone to hear, cursing Tom loudly as she watched the bacon cook through. She did not feel hungry, but a few more pieces of bacon never hurt anyone. She cracked an egg into the skillet for good measure and forgot all about the foreman and his craziness.

The telegram and its extreme urgency had put all thoughts of food aside for the foreman as he dashed out to the stable for his horse. This wire cried out a warning. He had to get off a response immediately, and he cursed himself for not having reacted sooner and for not going with Ki and Miss Jessie.

Of course, Miss Jessie had ridden into danger before, Tom reflected, and had always come back safely. He had been with Alex Starbuck since before little Jessica was born and looked upon her as his goddaughter. He realized she was a grown woman and could take care of herself, but the Circle Star's foreman knew there were some things that even a fighter as proficient with the martial arts and weapons as Ki couldn't protect her from.

Tom Hollander felt a grinding knot deep in his stomach. Full of recriminations, he swore to himself all the way to the telegraph office. He knew he could never forgive himself if anything happened to Miss Jessie—or to Ki. They were his family, and he felt as if he had betrayed them by allowing them to go without him. Heading straight into Indian Territory was foolhardy at best, but a beautiful young blonde with only one man to stand by her just cried out for the worst kind of trouble.

10

★
Chapter 3

"We're heading straight into Indian Nations territory," Ki cautioned as he and Jessica Starbuck rode side by side along the barren plains land. "It might have been safer to follow the Chisholm Trail, going through the Five Civilized Tribes land, instead of this Western Trail."

Jessie said, "It's too far to go around the Nations, and this trail takes us just a few miles to the east of Harcourtville." She stood in her stirrups to gain a better vantage point. "There may be clusters of Indians all through this region, but they're accustomed to trail herds and white people."

"Yes, but not many yellow-haired squaws," Ki said, a half-laugh behind his warning.

Jessie squinted into the sun as she lifted the brim of her hat slightly to wipe her forehead; road dust and perspiration darkened the broad monogrammed handkerchief. She tucked the piece of civilized luxury into the sleeve of her blouse and said, "We'll just have to be more careful than usual and keep ourselves alert. With any luck, we'll make it all the way to Harcourtville without sighting anyone—or anyone sighting us."

Ki's sorrel whinnied and shied to the left. "It might already be too late," Ki rasped as he tried to see through the thick underbrush on the top of a dusty knoll off to the right not more than a dozen yards.

11

As Jessica leaned forward, reaching for her Winchester, a *whoosh* whizzed by her ear. Her palomino reared and bolted forward, carrying her along at a fierce pace. She grabbed for the reins she had dropped when the mount lurched. Ki fired his rifle blindly into the sagebrush around the knoll as an arrow grazed the back of his saddle. His sorrel made a mighty attempt to overtake Jessie's panicked steed as Ki concentrated his rifle fire on the ridge of the knoll, but Ki had wrapped the reins around the horn so tightly that the gelding came to a complete stop and stood stock still.

A familiar primitive war cry changed in midwhoop to a howl of agony as Ki's random rifle bullets pelted the ridge and the growth above it. The Japanese-American martial-arts master wheeled his horse around and headed for the knoll. In an ambush, there had been no time to use his *shuriken,* since no clear target could be seen. And, as it turned out, a simple scattering of bullets had taken care of the problem—unless more Indians hid from view, waiting to pick off Jessie and him.

Even before he reached the top of the knoll, Ki heard the frantic hoofbeats of a single riderless horse racing away, probably toward home. Rifle ready, he slipped from his mount and rushed the top of the hill. A sprawled body, war paint masking the face, lay in a twisted heap amid the sagebrush. Ki nudged a lean motionless thigh with the toe of his moccasin, but his foot met with no response.

Jessica's young palomino trotted up the ridge, now completely under control. "How many?" she asked, looking off into the distance as the spooked runty hammerhead kicked up dust far to the east, its clubbed tail barely visible against the horizon.

"From all evidence, just the one," Ki said as he stepped gingerly around the painted bushwacker's body.

"Comanche," she said, yanking the arrow from Ki's cantle and inspecting the feathers. "Nasty lot."

Ki nodded emphatically. "I don't think we have much to worry about—unless this fella's horse brings a search party." His hand protecting his eyes from the sun's afternoon glare, Ki gazed off into the distance, trying to pick up the dusty trail of the runaway Indian pony. "It all depends on how far away their camp is." He continued to stare off into the barren land, checking thoroughly in all directions for dust and riders.

Jessica Starbuck surveyed the area. "It might be a good idea to put as much distance as possible between this ridge and us— just in case." She adjusted her flat-crowned hat to guard her face from the sun's blazing rays and motioned for Ki to mount up. "Let's head for that creek off to the northwest and ride the stream for a few miles to make sure we're not followed." She tilted her head toward the fallen warrior. "He may have been a loner, but he might also have been a scout. Let's get out of here—now."

Before the lovely blonde had finished speaking, Ki swung his lithe frame up into the saddle and urged his sorrel off toward the creek at a gallop. Jessie kept a beat behind him, acknowledging Ki's superior tracking and evasion techniques. The two guided their long horses up the middle of the sparkling stream, only slowing slightly as horseshoe met rounded boulder. They both knew this would not be the time for one of them to stumble and possibly sustain injury, yet it seemed imperative that they get away fast.

While the going proved slower than Jessie or Ki had expected, overhanging branches of trees and bushes hid them from view of anyone beyond the creek's banks. A few miles upstream, the waters cut into the land, creating a narrow eroded gorge that went deeper and deeper. They could no longer see the plains, but no one could see them unless standing at the canyon's edge.

Swaying to the rhythm of their steeds' careful progress, Jessie and Ki sank into deep thought. Ki kept his eyes on the creek and the canyon walls to either side, glancing up ahead while checking peripherally. He had been assigned to protect young Jessica Starbuck, heiress to the Lone Star fortune, so many years before, yet the responsibility had seemed almost a part of him. Even had her father not asked, Ki would gladly have laid down his life for Alex Starbuck's daughter in any case.

At the hoot of an owl, Ki raised his hand, signaling for Jessie to stop and arm herself. He motioned her to leave the creek to

13

the right, and he pulled his sorrel's reins to lead the gelding off to the left. Both riders slid from their mounts in silence, straining to hear the calls of birds ahead. Jessie nodded to Ki, letting him know she heard the calls and recognized them as foreign to the time of day. Ki's keen hearing and unusual awareness had kept them from riding into another ambush.

The wide banks of the creek made it easy to tether their horses to sturdy bushes, and the two made their way upcreek on foot. Each hugged the canyon wall, circling between bushes and around trees. Mindful not to step on twigs or break branches, the two converged on a shallow pool bordered by big boulders. Off beyond, crystal-clear water cascaded into the pool from two large rocks. The birdcalls seemed to be coming from behind the boulders. Jessie and Ki crept around quietly, Winchesters at the ready, until they had a clear view of the painted bushwackers lying in wait. Covered in full war paint, the three Comanches stared straight downstream, obviously waiting for the pair of paleskins to ride into their ambush.

Jessie froze and waited for Ki to make the first move. He employed a time-consuming *ninja* approach, sneaking up on the assailants silently from the left side. Although the rocks blocked her view, Ki's amazing maneuver was so familiar that Jessie could almost see Ki as he slipped noiselessly along under cover of brush and boulders. She recognized the familiar *whir* of a flying *shuriken* as the deadly metal throwing star bit through the air and into the flesh of one of the ambushers.

Winchester in hand, Jessie poised and spun around to her right. She brought her rifle up and was about to squeeze the trigger when she saw that all three Indians lay sprawled on the rocks. One, his mouth open in a soundless scream, bled profusely from a gash in his throat. The other two, also apparently dead, lay with heads twisted in unnatural positions. Ki stood behind them, staring off into the underbrush with his usual intensity.

"Do you think that's all of them?" Jessie asked as she looked around.

"I don't hear anything," Ki said. "This may be the rest of the advance party, or it may be all of them." He motioned for Jessie to follow and wandered farther upstream till he found the Comanches' tethered, unsaddled horses.

Ki tied the rope reins of the first horse tighter to the bushes, making sure that while the animal could reach water, it would take a long while before it left the canyon. Jessie understood and did the same. When all three horses were secured, they headed back toward their own horses, keeping as close to the canyon wall as possible for needed cover.

Ki said urgently, "The less time we spend around here, the better."

"I'm right behind you," Jessie called quietly.

Ki said over his shoulder, "Hopefully, by leaving their horses tied where they are, we'll buy some time. If the horses wander back to camp too soon, someone will head out after us while they can still pick up our trail. But if neither these Comanches nor their ponies return, and there do prove to be others, no one will know whether these braves are still following us or not."

"Good thinking." Jessie ducked under branches, hopping from boulder to boulder downstream. Since they no longer had to worry about making noise, they could go straight for their mounts.

Jessica and Ki found their palomino and sorrel right where they had tethered them. Ki walked his red gelding downstream to where the gorge began and out into the open before mounting. From the horse's back, he could see farther. He listened as Jessie stood motionless, waiting for him to survey the land. Finally, Ki nodded, and Jessie slipped her boot into the stirrup and pulled herself up onto the light cream-colored young mare.

Ki took off at a gallop with Jessie close behind. Without a word between them, they both knew it would be wise to get out of there as quickly as possible. They had to put as many miles as possible between them and another attack before they could make camp for the night. They also realized they would probably have to eat a cold supper, since a fire would only serve as a glowing invitation to further attacks.

Jessie felt grateful that Tom had prepared their long horses for them, since the steeldusts had a much greater endurance for riding all-out than did their favorite steeds. The two galloped along for several miles without breaking gait. The sun dipped into the west and slid under the horizon before the two riders pulled in their reins and slowed to a trot. Ki had kept an eye out for dust behind them, but they seemed to have been alone.

As dusk made ready to plunge them into darkness, Ki and Jessie brought their mounts to a stop near a hillock. Two enormous oak trees spread their branches out for yards on either side of the crest. Ki slipped to the ground and tied his sorrel to a low-hanging branch. Jessie swung her leg over the horn and jumped down next to him.

Ki climbed to the top of the hill and looked in all directions. The light had been replaced by deepening shadows that grew longer and darker by the moment. Jessie tethered her palomino next to Ki's horse and dug into her pack for some food. She knew even before Ki said anything that they would have a cold meal. The weather was warm, and if they took turns sleeping, they would not need a fire to protect them from night animals and predators.

"You take the first watch," Ki said as he climbed back down the hill. "I want to be awake before dawn—just in case those Comanches are still after us. All right?"

Jessie smiled as she pulled out her bedroll and spread it on the ground. "That's fine. After supper, you can stretch out and catch some sleep. I still feel wide awake, anyway. When the north star and the moon dip below the horizon, I'll wake you."

Ki unrolled his blanket and took a large hunk of beef jerky from Jessie. The two listened to the sounds of night on the prairie as they chewed on the sticks of dried meat and drank from their canteens.

Jessie watched Ki wrap himself in his blanket as she climbed the hillock for a good vantage point. She crouched at the foot of one of the huge oaks and settled in to enjoy the vivid display of heavenly sky lights. No matter how many times she saw stars appear in a darkened sky, she never ceased to thrill at the sight. Before long, the deepening blue of the world's ceiling would turn to black while millions of candles flickered on, crossing the sky at a remarkable rate of speed. Jessica Starbuck smiled and, although completely alert, welcomed the nightly light show.

16

At about one in the morning, Jessie crept over to Ki's blanket and whispered his name. She waited, but he didn't move; his breathing remained deep and rhythmic. She took his shoulder and gently shook it, and his breathing stopped completely. Before he could make a move, she whispered his name again, forestalling an attack.

"I must have been more tired than I realized," Ki said quietly as he pulled himself out of the blanket and stretched his muscles. "I really slept hard."

Jessie laughed. "You had me worried for a moment when you didn't stir. At least I won't have to worry about your falling asleep on watch—that was a deep sleep." She slipped into her bedroll and tucked the blanket around her. " 'Night," she called as she snuggled and stretched and fell quickly to sleep.

Ki took a long sip from his canteen before ascending the hill again. He propped himself against the trunk of the bigger tree and listened to the night noises. He hoped the dawn would come and bring them nothing but a beautiful new day—no savage bushwackers. He propped his Winchester across his legs and watched the stars make their way across the black heavens.

Some time later, down in the flatland, Jessie woke with a start. She had no idea how long she had slept, but the sun had not peeked out of the east yet, so it was still very early. A beetle, or something with several legs, had skittled across her face from chin to cheek, bringing her to consciousness with a sudden jolt. She sat up on one elbow and looked for Ki, but he seemed nowhere in sight. Her eyes tried to penetrate the darkness to catch his silhouette against the stars, but he wasn't where he should have been. He should have been up on the crest of the hill—but he wasn't.

Because Jessie had kept watch at the base of the huge tree trunk just at the crest of the hill, she had expected that Ki would do the same. Where was he? she wondered. She threw the blanket off and had started to get up when she heard a harsh whisper from above.

"Go back to sleep. It isn't dawn yet."

Looking almost straight up, she saw a dark shadow blanking out some of the stars. Ki was in the branches of the other tree, watching out for her from directly overhead. She pulled her broad-brimmed hat over her face, to discourage night crawlers and hopefully block dawn's first rays, and chuckled to herself as she drifted off for the second time that evening.

"Good night, again," she slurred just before continuing her interrupted dream.

Ki smiled but spoke no response. If an attack were to come, he would be ready, in the last place redskins would expect to find him—up in a tree. His Winchester, propped against the tree trunk, gleamed a dull blue in the starlight of predawn. Ki wanted ambushers to think he had left his post to stretch his legs or relieve himself. He had set up an ambush of his own.

Were there more Comanches? Ki wondered as he looked out over the darkness. He heard a tiny creature skitter across the brush, and a predatory bird swoop down. His keen ears picked up the rip of talons into fur and flesh and one final squeak of anguish. The endless food chain—one living being providing sustenance for another. Only people hunted for pleasure.

As the first rays of sunlight in the east broke over the hillock, painting grays and purples in to blend with the black of receding night, morning birds chirped brightly and several small animals dashed from their hiding places, scurrying to a more secure spot. Too much movement—more critters than should be running at that time of the day, Ki thought as he strained to listen even more closely. The small furry creatures froze in their tracks, and most of the birds went silent—all but a group of morning larks.

Ki noticed the call of four distinct morning larks, one on each side of the hillock—east, west, north, and south. Not coincidence, and definitely not birds. The Comanche braves let one another know when they were in place and ready to attack. Ki poised on his broad perch, hoping the warriors would not look up. The entire area, bathed in deep shadows but growing lighter by the minute, would soon be overrun by bright sunlight, and any element of surprise Ki or the Comanches had set up would be gone.

As Ki readied a *shuriken,* the painted redstick from the west crawled silently on his belly toward Jessica Starbuck's blanket, tomahawk in hand. Still several yards away, the Comanche approached stealthfully while another pulled himself up the hillock toward Ki's waiting Winchester.

With a bloodcurdling whoop, both braves leaped at their targets. The one on the hillock grabbed Ki's rifle and pointed it at Jessie's hat. The painted warrior with the tomahawk brought down his weapon full force on the hat just as the brave with the newly acquired Winchester pulled the trigger several times. The brave with the rifle fell back from the force of the shots, and a scream of pain from the blanket riddled the early morning air.

★

Chapter 4

At the sound of rifle shots and a blood-chilling scream from the bedroll, several shadowy figures let loose savage war whoops and rushed the foot of the hillock. The *zing* of a fast-moving object preceded a cry of agony as Ki's throwing star caught one painted shape by the neck and ripped a hole in the vital portion of the throat. The fatally wounded warrior glanced up seconds before his body collapsed in a heap, a look of surprise gone glazed.

Two Comanche braves, tomahawks raised, rushed over the crest of the hill, circling the massive tree trunks and using them for cover. Bursts of rifle fire caught first one and then the other, hurtling their painted bodies backward. A subdued glow from the rising sun still hidden by the horizon cast an orange hue on the trees and those under it. Shadows grew shorter, and figures became more visible.

From his vantage point in the heavy branches of one of the two huge oaks, Ki surveyed the raiding party. The dawn light made the streaks of white and yellow war paint stand out eerily against the deep gray of the early-morning western sky. Five down and three to go—unless there were more he couldn't see. An arrow whizzed past his head, almost grazing his shoulder, as he leaped from the branch and planted both feet on the ground before delivering a deadly whirling *tobi-geri* kick. Ki's heel

21

landed squarely on the Comanche's jaw, snapping the warrior's neck instantly.

From off to the side, another painted brave came at Ki with knife in hand, a whoop of hatred bellowing forth. Ki spun around and let loose his own cry of combat as his foot jarred the knife from the warrior's hand with the audible crack of a splintered wrist. The Comanche warrior fell to his knees as the heel of Ki's hand rammed the brave's nasal cartilage into his skull. A limp body crumpled at Ki's feet with a *thunk*.

The last of the war party came at Ki from behind, rushing the tall *te* master with both knife and tomahawk. Ki heard the war cry just in time and made ready to wheel and kick, but the slumped body at his feet blocked the way as the lone Comanche barreled down on him. Ki turned his torso to meet the oncoming enemy with fighting fingers ready, but the crack of a Colt revolver cut through the chill of early morning, echoing across the plains and creating a crimson hole between the warrior's startled eyes.

Ki watched the last painted brave fall back, tomahawk and knife still clenched in his hands. The tall Japanese-American smiled and looked up into the branches. "Well, that was worth losing a little sleep over, wasn't it?" he said as he raised his arms.

Light as a kitten, Jessica Starbuck slipped into his waiting hands and righted herself on the ground. All around, bodies of painted Comanches stained the knoll and shaded area beneath the trees. "Yes, you were right. But thank goodness they waited until nearly dawn before their attack. I got a few good hours."

Jessie glanced at her blanket and the grisly body sprawled across it. Ki shook his head and laughed sardonically as the honey-blonde's eyes followed his gaze up to the crest of the hillock.

"Victim of my Winchester." He pointed to the top of the knoll. "His friend up there must have mistaken this one for you—he shot him twice."

She tugged the blanket and tarpaulin out from under the slain Comanche. "It was nice of him not to bleed on my blanket," she said solemnly as she inspected it more closely. What started out as a smile disappeared when she lifted the tomahawk buried

22

in her hat. "Oops! Looks as if I would have been scalped had I actually been sleeping there when they attacked."

Ki held up the intact flat-crowned hat and examined the large indentation. He smiled wryly. "Lucky for you he didn't come at your bedroll with a knife or a gun, or you'd have an open-air sun hat."

Jessie looked around at the carnage and shuddered. "I wonder if there are any more of them out there waiting to waylay us. I hope this is all there is of this raiding party."

Ki shook his head. "I have a feeling this is it." He smiled. "Of course, I could be wrong—how about a look from the highest point?"

From the crest of the hillock, Jessica looked out over the plains, searching for any human movement, but saw none. Some bison grazed off in the distance, and a hawk or two surveyed the land from a floating circle. She pulled her hat brim lower to cut out the sun's glare, but all looked peaceful. As she bounced down the hill, she rubbed her hands together. "I guess it's safe to make a fire now. We could both use some good, strong coffee. But perhaps we should move along to some other site—and get away from the stench of death."

The pair packed up their bedrolls and prepared for the next leg of their journey northward. A mile or so up the trail, they stopped long enough to make a fire. Ki piled a few dead branches and kindled the fire while Jessie poured water from her canteen into a battered old coffee pot. While the coffee brewed, they tried to understand the events of the past day or so.

When the coffee smelled ready, they each poured a cup and kicked out the fire. They consolidated what water they both had left into one canteen, poured the fresh hot coffee into the other canteen, and rode off with full cups in hand. They sipped the dark, exhilarating brew in silence as they left the scene of death far behind.

Jessie wondered to herself if there might not be a connection between the Comanches' attempts on them and their trip north. When she and Ki had discussed it while waiting for the coffee to brew, they had finally concluded that the war party probably came upon them by accident. Ki had reminded her that the Comanche tribes had split, with the Kiowa Comanches staying north and the rest heading far south, almost to the Mexican border. Neither she nor Ki had any idea which branch the aggressors had belonged to, but they had agreed the warriors were probably just territorial renegades with nothing whatsoever to do with the Harcourts and their urgent problem.

As they rode along, Jessie's mind ran over the attacks again and again to see if there was any possible clue to a link, no matter how tenuous, between the Harcourts and the Comanches. Without all the information, there was no way to know.

Deep in his own thoughts, Ki focused on Hubert Harcourt and his first meeting with the man years ago in San Francisco. Ki's reminiscence returned him to the days following that fairly uneventful meeting, and his memory scratched around the edges for some idea of what he and Jessie now faced with the plea from Harcourt's daughter. But the whispers of the past flung him even farther back—back to the day he first met Alex Starbuck.

As far back as Ki could remember, there had always been an Alexander Starbuck. There had never been a time when the tall, blond, extremely handsome man had not existed in Ki's life. Ki's father, an American naval officer, had become captain of the merchant ship *Lady Light* out of Yokohama. Alex Starbuck owned the *Lady Light*, along with many other ships, and considered Ki's father a very close friend.

The respect Ki felt for his father's good friend went far beyond normal bounds—Alex Starbuck's heroic start in the world of finance and industry proved enough to stagger most people's imaginations, but his good-heartedness, thoughtfulness, and generosity seemed almost overwhelming. Ki's father had related to his young son many of the adventures he had shared with Alex Starbuck, always starting with his friend's humble beginnings. And Ki never tired of hearing how Alex got his start—it seemed so much like the heroes in the novels by that new American author Horatio Alger.

As a young man, Alex Starbuck had worked on the San Francisco waterfront. After some months, the young man had saved enough money to open his own little curio shop of oriental imports. The Gold Rush had padded men's pockets, and they could easily afford exotic trinkets shipped in from the Orient. To his surprise, Alex found he had a knack for knowing what people wanted and providing it. His shop grew as customers flocked; soon he could afford to buy his own small broken-down ship and thus cut out the middle man. His one frail vessel plied the Pacific Ocean between the Orient and San Francisco, bringing loads of sought-after Eastern imports to the Barbary Coast.

As Alex Starbuck's coffers swelled, so did his fleet. With an accumulation of ships came an abundance of funds, which Alex seemed to innately know how to invest to make the most of his wealth. The young man knew it would cost less to build his own ships than to lease or buy them; so he started a shipyard on San Francisco Bay, not far from the pier where he first began as a dockworker.

When iron-hulled ships proved more seaworthy than their wooden counterparts, Alex converted his shipyard to metal. As steel became more popular, he changed over to this stronger blend of ores; then he bought a steel mill to provide his shipyard's metal. Acquisition and expansion kept him buoyant, and the end of the Civil War, known then as the War Between the States, produced an industrial explosion that rocked the entire country. Alex Starbuck felt fortunate to get in on the ground floor and soon became one of the country's most promising tycoons of industry and finance—a heroic figure larger than life, the beginning of the Starbuck legend.

In the shortest time possible, Alex Starbuck's fortune had allowed him to expand his holdings. From one coast to the other, Starbuck properties grew and prospered. His name and reputation were known around the world.

Ki's mother, a beautiful young woman from one of Japan's most noble families, recounted tales of Alex-san in her husband's absence each time the naval captain sailed to America on one of his many trips. When Ki's father went down with his ship, the maternal family showed its true blue-blood colors by banishing Ki, who disgraced them with his "tainted" half-American blood. They let him know there was no place for an Amerasian in Japan or in their hearts.

Against his mother's wishes, Ki left home and entered a monastery, where he studied to become a *karateka* master—a warrior of bare-handed combat. After years of constantly improving his skills of unarmed battle, where anything from a broom handle to a stone could become a lethal weapon, the rejected young child grew in stature and strength and became a true *te* master—a man of great inner power, whose patience and understanding guided him while his vast martial-arts skill protected him. Tall, lean, and dark, he stood out in a land of shorter people. Although half-Asian, he was looked upon with suspicion by those who did not know him.

With the lessons he had learned at the feet of the Master, Ki fought many battles alongside comrades who also railed against the expansionist Japanese elite. His future had seemed all but set as a mongrel warrior fighting for his people's rights, but his path crossed with Alex Starbuck once again, thus changing his life forever. Ki accepted a position with the Starbuck empire, and Alex took his close friend's cherished son back to America and a future he could never have dreamed possible in his wildest fantasies.

Already unsurpassed as a *te* master—his concentration and determination at the monestary had placed him high above all others—Ki proved as intelligent as he was skilled in combat. Alex valued Ki's keen mind and pure inner qualities molded from years of the pain of prejudice and rejection. Before long, Ki became Alex's right arm and bodyguard, and a member of the Starbuck family. Although Alex had wed young, he had married well. When Alex's wife came ready to give birth to the Starbuck heir, Ki vowed to protect the Starbucks with his life.

Ki consoled Alex, who, when his beautiful young wife died in childbirth, stoically wrestled with a tragedy that would crush most men. Alex suffered and blamed himself, and seemed bound to throw aside everything he had accumulated.

Ki said, "Your loss is incontrovertible, and it produces more pain than any one man should have to bear."

Alex merely sobbed in self-pity.

"I loved her, too, as you well know." Ki smiled sadly as his voice softened. "My so-called aristocratic family turned their

26

back on me because they considered me a half-caste, but your beautiful wife—of high birth herself—accepted me as part of the family, looking not at my physical differences but at my heart and soul."

Alex smiled wanly as Ki's words hit home.

Ki pointed out that Alex's wife had forfeited her life for their daughter, Jessica, and would want to live through her—little Jessie would be an extension of her. Such reasoning yanked Alex from the depths of despair when he realized that little Jessie would some day inherit the Starbuck empire and fortune and needed at least one parent. Ki suggested that although Alex would now have to be both mother and father to this adorable infant, Ki would add his love and caring to raising the little girl.

From that time on, Alex and Ki worked toward the day when all would be turned over to Jessie. When she was old enough to be sent away to school, Ki pined almost as much as did her father. But distractions took their minds off the honey-blond beauty—if only temporarily and in short spurts. Alex acquired mines, forests, brokerage and commodities houses, banks, and—as progress forged on—railroads and freight lines. The benevolent Starbuck tentacles reached to all corners of America, while the Circle Star Ranch, the heart of the Starbuck empire, grew in size and riches at an alarming rate.

European industrial and financial interests had watched Alex Starbuck's growth with a justifiably wary eye, waiting to see if his genius for expansion might become a threat to their plans. For several years, the European powers and the Starbuck empire coexisted relatively peaceably. One vicious European cartel, however, viewed as a flagrant act of hostility Alex's rejection of their frequent invitations for him to join forces with them.

Alex saw the malicious cartel's overtures as attempts to take over America, and he put all his power and resources into the financial battle to keep all foreign cartels out of this country. He felt America had suffered enough at the hands of the Rebs during the War Between the States, and he felt honor bound to protect the land he loved from being invaded by unscrupulous forces.

Already smarting from their loss of power in the shrinking European domain they had once reigned over, the treacherous cartel took aggressive action by sending in paid assassins to blast Alex Starbuck out of existence. It took an ambush while Ki was lured elsewhere to finally drop the young American tycoon.

Jessica Starbuck, far away in boarding school, had rushed back to Texas to stand beside Ki at her father's funeral. Her first act as heir to the Starbuck empire had been to hunt down her father's murderers and bring them and the entire cartel to justice—her justice. Not easily vanquished, the cartel survived one attack after another. But Jessie, being very much her father's daughter, finally defeated them after many separate battles.

One by one, Jessie had sought out each of the men sent to kill her father, and with Ki's devoted assistance, she had brought them all to a much higher court than any American judge ever sat on. After all the assassins had been punished to Jessica's satisfaction, the young beauty turned her wrath on the vicious cartel and succeeded in dismantling it completely.

In doing so, Jessica Starbuck had gained a reputation as the brave young woman who walked in her father's footsteps, championing the underdog and the little people—and possessing the wherewithal to accomplish almost anything. Her courage and determination, coupled with her father's fortune, seemed most formidable.

The lovely daughter of Alex Starbuck had explained on many an occasion, "There are far too many people in this world who need help the law cannot or will not bring. Justice, ethics, and equality are not always our God-given right." She determined to devote herself to righting injustices, and she put the full power of all her assets—physical, mental, and financial—to bear on each situation.

Ki knew Jessie Starbuck entertained a bittersweet memory of her father and his legendary accomplishments. How proud she had been of the only parent she had ever known, and how distraught she had been to lose him. As the two rode quickly toward Harcourtville to answer another in a long list of cries for help that never went unheeded, Ki focused on the honey-blond curls that tumbled down the heiress's back as her palomino swayed in front of his sorrel. The dignity of that proud back and her finishing-school posture seemed almost out of place astride a horse and clad in a leather vest and bright-colored shirt.

What had he been thinking about? Ki wondered. What had started him off on the memory trail? Oh, yes—Hubert Harcourt, he thought. Halleybelle's urgent telegram had brought Jessie and him on the road and hurtled them into the malevolent ambush by the Comanche war party. Any connection? He hoped not.

★

Chapter 5

Graham Greenleaf stretched out his long legs and tried to make himself a little more comfortable in Widow Hammond's massive living room. The air felt stifling, with a huge fire going strong in the large stone fireplace. Greenleaf knew from years of experience that most older women seemed to love the heat—it never got hot enough for them. Perhaps, he thought quite often, age thins the blood. He pulled at the paper collar around his neck, hoping to find a little relief from the heat without tearing it. His three-piece broadcloth suit felt slightly damp. He hoped the moisture would not show, since sweating showed possible duplicity.

The gold-colored, embroidered and hand-tufted settee had been built for a tall man's proportions, and the suave swindler planned to enjoy the soft seat for as long as possible. The hard saddle of his rented bay gelding caused him no end of pain. And the wooden seat of a buckboard would be no softer or more inviting.

"Amanda—I may call you Amanda?" he said grandly, fiddling with his long gold watch chain. "Time flits by so quickly when I'm with you, but I must be on my way soon. You know I really would rather stay, but . . . " He waited for her protest.

"But, Graham!" The sixty-year-old woman's lower lip quivered as her eyes pleaded with him to stay. "More coffee?" she asked as she took the pot from the fireplace and poured the dark brew into his cup. "And another biscuit?" She shoved the plateful of lumpy cookies under his nose. "I made them for you, you know."

"Amanda, you spoil me." Graham Greenleaf plucked two cookies from the plate, depositing one on his saucer next to the cup. As he munched gratefully on the cookie and sipped the strong liquid to help dissolve the almost inedible biscuit, he managed a grin of appreciation. "Truth be told, my dear, you've done far too much for me as it is. And I know I have overstayed my welcome."

Amanda Hammond shook her head until her salt-and-pepper curls slapped her pale cheeks. "Never—you could never overstay . . . you will always be welcome here!" She flushed and looked down demurely at the lap of her powder blue velveteen-and-lace frock. "Besides, I want to buy more of that wonderful Henerow Corporation stock. You do have more, don't you?" Her large blue eyes searched his face for signs of rejection but saw only surprise.

Graham Greenleaf choked on his coffee and coughed until his eyes watered. Putting down the blue-and-white cup and saucer, he blew his nose noisily into a large discolored handkerchief.

He cleared his throat with a little drop of coffee and asked, "*More* stock? But the other day you told me you had only so much money to spend on outside investments. You said the cash you gave me for the shares of Henerow Corporation stock was all you had—your life savings, didn't you say?" He left the other questions unspoken.

She nodded, smiling brightly. "Oh, I know. And I spoke the truth—I could not part with any more cash. But I have found a way to loosen up more money so I can take advantage of this marvelous opportunity." Her eyes begged him to sell her more.

Behind Amanda's pathetic plea was a look of extreme determination. Graham Greenleaf's mind whirled as the swindler tried to understand what was going on. Amanda Hammond was the fifth widow in the past two months who had asked to buy more stock than originally agreed upon, rather than less as most people did. The traveling confidence man had been accustomed to following his soft-sell approach with a strong closing to ward off second thoughts and cold feet. A professional of almost thirty years as a flimflam man, he had never run into a situation quite like this one. Never had anyone ever insisted on buying *more* stock than he offered.

The dapper man squirmed in his seat and yanked at his reddish mustache. "Amanda, my dear, I do not want to take advantage of you. You already told me that you could afford no more than what you've already purchased." He pulled at his mustache so hard, a few bristles came out in his fingers as he looked around to see if the sheriff or the marshal might be eavesdropping, just waiting to cuff him for fraud. "Besides," he said, his face brightening, "I have no more stock certificates."

"Oh, no!" the widow wailed. "I'm too late! I knew it—I just knew it! Oh, please, Graham—please, for me?" Her large blue eyes brimmed with tears.

Graham Greenleaf watched the spectacle with unabashed amazement. This woman was actually crying because he said he was out of stock certificates! Something seemed very wrong, but he had not a clue to this recent demand on his stock. Gawd, truth be told, if the stock really were real—I'd be rich! he thought. Of course, the amount of money he had taken in from the last few pigeons was enough to keep him in booze, broads, and betting for a good long time.

"Oh, please!" Amanda Hammond cooed softly, trying her feminine wiles on the lanky man as she tried to mask her desperation.

"Truly, my dear, I have no more stock certificates with me." He laughed loudly. "After all, I can't just manufacture them, can I?"

She tittered at the humor of his words. "Well, of course not! But your company must have more shares at the home office. Couldn't you wire the Henerow Corporation and ask them for more? I'm sure they would never turn you down—not you."

The good-looking flimflam man held his breath and made an instantaneous decision to go along with the woman. He had no idea what might be going on, but so far on this trip through

33

Harcourt County, he had managed to stay out of the grasp of the law. It would do no harm to sell her more stock if she wanted it that badly. But, truth be told, he really was out of certificates. And he had also run out of the paper to print more on.

"All right, my lovely, I will contact the main office and have them send more stock certificates. How could I ever refuse you anything?" He took her wrinkled hand in his and placed a dry kiss on her knuckles.

Amanda giggled as his reddish mustache tickled her flesh. "Esmeralda Harcourt was right, rest her soul. You *are* wonderful. I am so pleased she suggested you see me before she passed on."

Another reason to get out of here quickly! the swindler thought as he squeezed the widow's hand and stood. "Truth be told, my lovely, were I not to bring back more stock certificates to you, I would be forced to think up another excuse to see you again."

"Oh, Graham—"

"Now, Amanda, I really must be going. I will telegraph the company headquarters immediately and bring you as many more certificates as you want." He pulled on his riding coat and reached for his hat. "By the way, how many more shares do you want, my dear?"

Amanda Hammond blinked stubby gray lashes at him. "Well, I have no head for business, but . . . " She pulled at the lace hankie in her hands, hesitant to reply. Finally gathering enough courage, she said, "May I please have, say, two thousand more?"

"Two thou—" Graham Greenleaf swallowed hard and tried to keep from choking on his own saliva. "Whatever you say, my dear. But by the time I get back with the certificates, the price of a share may have gone up."

Amanda Hammond shook her head, causing her curls to rock back and forth again. "Oh, I don't care. I can manage. Besides, I know it's a good investment! I just know it!" Her eyes shone brightly. "It's worth any price!"

The puzzled confidence man's heart sank. What was happening here? Something had gotten well out of control and he didn't like it. On the one hand, this old woman wanted to buy two thousand more shares! On the other hand, it might be a cleverly devised trap. To return with the newly printed shares tempted him, but he might wind up in jail or at the end of a rope.

Graham Greenleaf looked deep into Amanda's twinkling blue eyes and wondered what it was this old widow woman knew that he didn't.

★

Chapter 6

Neither Jessie nor Ki looked particularly happy when they finally arrived in Harcourtville shortly after noon and asked directions to the Harcourt ranch. The lengthy trip on horseback had taken its toll on them, and they each wanted more than anything else to slip into a hot tub and soak away the road dust and grit, and then to stretch out in a comfortable bed. While their journey had not lasted all that long, compared with some, the strain of constant danger from an unreasoning enemy and no relief from the blazing sun had kept them both on edge. They looked forward to allowing their muscles and nerves to relax—inside a cool ranch house.

The pair guided their horses through the dusty main street of Harcourtville to the blacksmith shop, the most likely place to ask about the Circle H Ranch. Jessie's palomino drank from a watering trough while Ki rode up to the sweating smithy standing in the shade of his shop. Sparks flew as the massive blacksmith brought a hammer down on a red-hot horseshoe. The resultant *clang* was all but deafening and echoed throughout the shop. Ki waited until the hammer hit and bounced several times before he cleared his throat. Apparently oblivious to Ki's presence, the large man picked up the horseshoe with metal tongs and plunged it into a rain barrel just outside the door. As steam hissed from the water, Ki cleared his throat more loudly.

"Excuse me, but would you know the way to the Circle H Ranch?" Ki asked once he had the muscular man's full attention.

The blacksmith stared up at Ki, taking in the Japanese-American's long, straight black hair and braided headband, his sparse mustache, and the foreign cut of his eyes. "Yeah, 'course I know the way," he said, as if dismissing Ki. The big man turned back to his work, shoving the shoe back into the glowing coals.

"Could you please tell us how to get there from here?" Ki persisted.

"Can't help yuh," the glistening smithy said without looking up. "Too busy—ain't got the time." He yanked the shoe from the fire onto the anvil again and brought the hammer down repeatedly, hard enough to drown out any possible conversation. The big man's thin lips became a determined slit, and his eyes looked only at the shoe he pounded.

Over the ear-shattering clatter, Ki yelled, "Where can we get directions?"

The big blacksmith's lips moved slightly, but Ki heard nothing. From the distortion of the large man's mouth, it appeared clear to Ki that whatever the man said was not what he would want to hear.

Ki turned his gelding and motioned for Jessie to follow as he led her away from the blacksmith shop at a trot. When they were far enough from the noise to be able to hear each other without the ringing of hammer on metal shoe disrupting them, they slowed the horses.

"Maybe he's just tired," Jessie said. "Let's stop at the cafe. We can get out of this sun and get ourselves a bite to eat while we find out how to get to the Circle H."

"Good idea."

Foot traffic in the town of Harcourtville appeared to be brisk—rough-looking men strolling along or picking their teeth on the steps of the raised wooden sidewalk in front of the saloon, women in gingham frocks hauling children by the hand, gentlemen in city suits headed for business meetings, grimy youngsters romping after a pet or eluding their mothers, prim ladies in linen gowns with matching parasols to protect themselves from the sun.

As Jessica Starbuck and Ki rode through the center of town, people stopped to stare. The men, for the most part, admired Jessie's honey-blond beauty and the seductively clinging cut of her blouse around such firm, round breasts; women gawked at a female in town in jeans—especially ones as tight and revealing as Jessie's—and a revolver in her holster, *astride* a horse. Most of the children noticed only Ki and created their own private fantasies about the exotic-looking stranger. One or two of the teenage girls gazed with envy at Jessica.

A block down the main street of town, across from the county jailhouse, Ki and Jessie came to Mom's Grub Shop. A sign in the window proclaimed, Tables for Ladies. They tethered their mounts at the hitching rack out front and climbed the wooden steps to the dingy little café. A bell jingled as Jessie pushed the door open, and mouth-watering aromas assailed her nostrils. Three customers lolled at two tables to the right of the door and paid no attention to the newcomers. A wiry young man seated at the counter turned to admire Jessie's sensuous beauty.

Someone from near the kitchen called out in a lyrical masculine voice, "Welcome to Mom's Grub Shop! And what be yer pleasure, me friends?"

It took a few moments for Jessie and Ki to accustom their eyes to the lack of bright sunlight at the back of the little restaurant. Finally, they saw a short, round man with a large orange mustache and a fringe of curly orange hair circling a shiny bald head. His bulging blue eyes sparkled as if he knew some deep, delicious secret and might share it with just the right person. A stained, once-white apron covered the jolly expanse of his belly, and his amiable grin stretched his magnificent mustache until the handlebars reached almost to his ears.

As Jessie and Ki sat at a table near the window, the plump little man ambled over and stood looking down at them, giving them full benefit of his gigantic dimples almost hidden by the magnificence of his mustache. It crossed Jessie's mind that were this man taller, and were his hair white—and had he a beard—he could very easily pass for Saint Nicholas at Christmastime.

"Thank you for the warmth of your welcome," Jessie said, offering him her sweetest smile—lowered lashes and all. The juicy pie on the counter caught her eye. "How about a piece of Mom's pie? And some coffee, please?"

The bald man nodded. "A hunk o' pie and a mug o' Mom's liquid poison, comin' right up, me darlin'." He looked at Ki. "And what about you, sir?"

Ki raised an eyebrow at the deference and friendliness and smiled. "Thank you. I'll have the same."

"Good choice! Pie's fresh outta the oven. I'll be right back." He hurried off to fill their order.

Jessie and Ki waited until they had finished the pie and coffee before asking directions to the Harcourt ranch. As the luscious honey-blonde put down her fork and brushed a crumb from her lips, she motioned the round man over. She shook her head emphatically.

"Now that was good pie!" she said. "Don't know when I've tasted better. You tell Mom I really enjoyed it."

Ki shot in, "It was indeed delicious." He looked around the all-but-empty diner, trying to see through the door to the kitchen. "Perhaps we could tell her ourselves."

The bald man's eyes crinkled with pleasure. "You already have!" He stuck out a meaty hand to Ki. "Michael O'Murray—Mom—at yer service! But you can be callin' me Mike if you'd rather."

Ki shook the proffered hand as Jessie laughed.

"And who be you?" he asked, his Irish lilt growing thicker by the moment.

"I'm Jessica and this is my associate Ki." She glanced over at the two men still eating their meal and lowered her voice slightly; the customer ogling her from the counter appeared well out of earshot. "We just rode in from Texas, and we're looking for the Circle H Ranch. You wouldn't happen to know how to get there, would you?"

"Now, of course I would. Ever'body knows the Harcourts—after all, wasn't this fine town named fer 'em . . . Harcourtville?" He stepped back and sized up Jessie, his eyes lingering for the briefest moment on her curvaceous body. Openly admiring the honey-blonde's bearing and regal posture, he said, "If I was a bettin' man, I'd say you was an old friend of Miss Halleybelle's." He chuckled. "Or, better yet, a 'close friend' of Mr. Bert Junior." He held his belly as he chuckled out loud. "But that'd be none o' my business, now would it, Miss Jessica?"

Jessie nodded. "You're right on both counts. I went to school with Halleybelle, and I can hardly wait to see Bert." She winked flirtatiously.

Mike whistled. "What a lucky man that Bert Junior is!" He nudged Ki on the shoulder and did a little jig. "Well, now, let's not let me be holdin' you up any longer then." As he cleared away the dishes, he gave them directions for the quickest route to the ranch.

Ki reached into his pocket for money, but Mike stopped him. "Now, please, let this be my welcome to the two of you." He winked at Jessie and said to Ki, "Next time, you can pay—and there'd better be a next time." He pulled on the end of his orange mustache as his sparkling eyes momentarily clouded over. "You know, 'twas terrible, old Mrs. Harcourt goin' to her final reward 'n' all. O'course, the grand lady had had her years, but I'm sure gonna miss her. That dear woman was such a love, ready for sainthood. I'm here to tell you that when me Bridey passed on, Mrs. Harcourt saved me from goin' down the big black hole. With all me kiddies grown and gone, I was that much alone, and the wonderful woman she was gave me somethin' to live for." Just as quickly as his somber tone had appeared, so it disappeared. He walked them to the door with a broad smile and a bounce in his step.

"We'll see you again soon," Jessie promised as she and Ki stepped out into the bright daylight. "Thank you—for everything."

"Sure, and it's my pleasure. Please be givin' me best to Miss Halleybelle and Mr. Bert Junior," he called as he closed the door behind them.

Jessie and Ki nodded and headed for their horses, but two rough-looking men who had been loitering by the hitching rack blocked their path. Both men had scraggly hair, dark beards,

41

and scars on their faces, and one had an ear missing. They wore their neckerchiefs high as though ready to pull over their faces at a moment's notice.

Unsavory! Jessie thought as she tried to sidestep them to get to her mount.

"Hey, beautiful—how's about a little drink at the saloon?" the man with one ear growled, his eyes openly undressing Jessie. "Dump the stupid damn Chink and let's have us a party."

Ki pulled Jessie behind him and confronted the men. "We don't want any trouble. We just want to get our horses and leave. Let us by."

The man with one ear threw back his head and laughed hard in Ki's face, a strong mixture of whiskey and vomit blended with sour tobacco on his breath nearly knocking over the tall Japanese-American. "Well, you dumb Chink, you don't seem to realize you already got trouble!" He looked at his buddy. "Don't he, Buck?"

"Yup!" said Buck as his hand edged toward a .44 Remington army revolver tied down in a legholster. His mouth bulging with chewing tobacco and slimy juice, he spat at Ki's feet for emphasis, splattering the *te* master's soft leather moccasins with a thick, dark brown fluid.

As the man with one ear reached past Ki for Jessie's wrist, Buck pulled his gun and aimed it at Ki. From off down the street, a young woman screamed and ran for cover. Children stopped playing and watched to see what would happen next. Mothers yanked little ones out of bullet range, and men backed off casually, trying not to appear too fainthearted. The town marshal, sitting with wooden chair propped against the brick wall of the jailhouse, slowly brought his seat upright and held his breath.

Ki took a step or two backward, which both toughs immediately read as an act of cowardice; they laughed and poked at each other. Jessie jumped back out of the way as Ki let out a piercing combat cry and, with the grace of a cat, swung his foot up in a swift curving *teri-gobi* kick, knocking Buck's revolver from his hand. But Ki's foot did not stop there. In a continuation of the swinging motion, he twirled, and his foot

42

kept right on going until it made audible contact with one-ear's bearded jaw.

"Goddamn it!" Buck bellowed as he watched his buddy lurch backward from the strength of Ki's kick. "You dirty sonuvabitch!" He came at Ki with bare hands ready to throttle. "I was only playin' afore, but now I'm gonna kill you, you rotten, stinkin' Chink!" With a howl of rage, he ran straight at Ki.

It took only a moment for Ki to regain his balance from the spinning kick, and he stood poised, waiting for the roughneck to come at him again. As the thug called Buck came close enough to reach for Ki's throat, the *te* master delivered a restrained *nakadata* blow to the tough's chest with his middle finger. A full blow would have pierced the man's chest cavity and burst the heart muscle. Ki held back and merely broke a few ribs, sending Buck sprawling in pain.

Mike, inside the little restaurant, pulled the door open to come to Jessie's rescue, but she motioned for him to get back inside. The town marshal across the street remained seated, apparently waiting for the outcome. Harcourtville's main thoroughfare seemed frozen in time, with everyone witnessing the confrontation from a safe distance or from behind windows or half-open doors.

The man with one ear shook his head to clear his mind and instantly regretted the action. He grabbed his chin in agony; his jaw felt broken, and he wisely did not attempt to speak. He offered his coughing friend a hand, and the two hulking thugs pulled themselves up to come at Ki as a team. The tall *te* master waited until they both stood, then he grabbed them by their neckerchiefs and flung their heads together with a solid *smaaat*!

The man called Buck crumpled into unconsciousness on the spot, while one-ear staggered and lost his balance, sprawling heavily against his senseless friend. It appeared obvious that the man with one ear wanted desperately to say something, but the pain from his jaw kept him from doing so. Instead, the large man growled menacingly from deep in his throat as he glared at Ki and pulled himself up on one knee, preparing to lunge at the *te* master again.

43

Jessie cocked her .45 Colt revolver loudly and said, "If I were you, I'd just stay there with your friend." She took Ki's outstretched hand and stepped over Buck's unconscious form. "It would be a whole lot more healthy down there for the time being." She glanced over at the lawman still seated in front of his jail. "Isn't that right, Constable?"

The lawman took off his ten-gallon hat, scratched his grizzled pate, and said, "Yes, ma'am, I reckon so." He turned his gaze back to the one-eared man. "Spike, you jes' stay there and tend to Buck." The marshal smiled tightly and tipped his hat to Jessie, his eyes tracing the curve of her bosom.

As soon as Jessie and Ki rode off, the town came back to life, and people went about their business as if nothing had happened. They stepped around Spike and Buck, and some of the younger boys, using finger six-shooters and fanning their thumbs, dared to pretend to shoot it out with the two wounded toughs. Spike ignored them and waited patiently for Buck to regain consciousness. Then the two roughnecks tried to figure out how to get themselves over to Doc Sawyer's without too much pain.

Not until she and Ki had mounted and headed out of town did Jessie holster her six-shooter. She looked back and waved at Mike standing on the sidewalk, half in and half out the grub shop door, grinning and tugging away at his long orange mustache.

"I hope there are more people like Mike and less like those two and the blacksmith in Harcourtville," she said, shaking her head.

"So do I."

★
Chapter 7

The sun dipped into the west as Jessie and Ki rode down the deeply rutted road out of town. A skunk's too-sweet scent wafted across their path as they urged their horses on. Overhead, two little birds squawked and darted at a large, free-floating hawk.

Ki shook his head as they followed Mike's directions to the Circle H Ranch. "Something bothers me about that situation back there. It just doesn't—"

"I felt it, too." Jessie nodded. "Why would a couple of roughnecks openly start something right in front of the law? And why didn't the marshal stop them when the first bully went for his revolver?"

"Exactly," Ki said. "They didn't appear to be stupid or drunk enough to pull something in the middle of town, and in front of a lawman . . . unless—"

"Unless they *could*!" Jessie finished Ki's sentence. "You're right. Come to think of it, I had my eye on the marshal part of the time, and I fully expected him to get up and say something or do something. But then when you went into action, I forgot about him." She tightened the drawstring on her hat as she picked up her palomino's gait. "Either those two toughs are related to someone powerful, or they work for someone powerful, or the law in this town is corrupt."

Ki quickened the pace still more. "I hope we're wrong, but I'm sure we'll find out when we get to the ranch."

There was no time to waste—Halleybelle's telegram had read *urgent*, and the the town's behavior suggested something was very wrong. Jessie and Ki rode the rest of the way in silence, hoping they were not too late for whatever it was that the Harcourts needed help with.

As Jessie and Ki approached the gated entrance to the Circle H Ranch, a shot rang out overhead. Before they could arm themselves, someone yelled, "Toss down your weapons and do it quick! No funny tricks or you'll be dead! Drop 'em now or else!"

Ki and Jessie did as the booming voice instructed. If the voice belonged to a bushwacker, they reasoned, they would both already be dead, dropped in their tracks. Slowly, carefully, they lowered their Winchester rifles by the barrels; then Jessie tossed down her Colt revolver.

"Yours, too, Chinaman!"

"I have no need for revolvers," Ki said to open space. A faint hint of lilac wafted to his nostrils, but he'd think about that later.

"Who are you?" the voice demanded.

Jessie dismounted and walked to the big wooden gate, shouting to whoever was on the other side in the bushes, "I'm Jessica Starbuck, and this is my friend and associate Ki. The Harcourts sent for us." Hoping the man behind the voice worked for the Harcourts, she added, "Ki knew Hubert Harcourt back in San Francisco when they both worked for my father, Alex Starbuck, and I attended school with Halleybelle Harcourt."

"Jesus! Jessica? Sorry for this, but it was necessary." A head popped up from behind a bush. The face of an extremely handsome young man came into view, and he approached. "Miss Starbuck, Ki, I'm really sorry. I'm Bert—Bert Junior— Hubert Harcourt's son. It's been so long, and you've changed so much I didn't recognize you, Jessie."

From behind a tree, another man stepped out and stood with a rifle cradled in his arms. Off beyond the bushes on the other side of the private road, two more men stepped into sight, weapons relaxed but ready. A slender figure in a gingham gown and apron dashed past Bert Junior, deep auburn hair hanging long in braids tied with material that matched the frock.

"Jessie!" the lovely young woman cried as she reached for the gate's lock. She pulled open the gate and ran into her friend's waiting arms. "Oh, Jessie, thank God you're here!" The two women hugged in silence for several moments, while the men looked one way and then another.

"Halleybelle Harcourt!" Jessie said, stepping back. "My goodness, just let me look at you." She surveyed her friend's figure, nodding approvingly. "You were such a pudgy little runt when I left school to run my father's business. And now you're slender and curvaceous and tall." Jessie looked more closely at her friend's face. "Were your lashes always that long and thick? I remember your round little face always seemed to be two huge rosy cheeks and two gigantic light-brown eyes. Oh, my, have you grown up!"

"And you haven't?" Halleybelle laughed and looked at Jessie in admiration. "Of course, you never went through an awkward stage. You were gorgeous from the moment I met you—and all you've done is become more lovely."

Jessie giggled, almost like a schoolgirl, and led her friend to Ki, who had slid off his gelding. "Halley, you know Ki—by reputation. I'm sure your father told you many tales of Ki's adventures, saving Father's life without weapons—a true *karateka*."

Ki took Halleybelle's hand gently in his and bent to kiss it, but merely brushed his lips over the soft, fragrant flesh. Ah, lilac—that answers that, he reflected as he breathed in deeply her alluring aroma and felt his loins heat up.

"Miss Harcourt," he said, a slight quaver to his usually well-regulated voice. He quickly looked over at the dark-haired young man behind her and extended his hand. "And I am pleased to meet you, too, Mr. Harcourt."

"Call me Bert, please, both of you. Ki, it's a real honor. And Jessica—it's a real pleasure." His light brown eyes, glowing with fine specks of gold, fixed on Jessie's huge green orbs and stared into their depths.

47

Jessie cleared her throat and smiled. She did not trust her voice.

Suddenly, Bert remembered the danger they were all in and insisted they get to the ranch house as soon as possible. Ki offered Halleybelle a lift up onto his sorrel, and Jessie put her hand out to help Bert mount behind her. Leaving the buckboard for the ranch hands, the two couples trotted off to the main house, while the other men blended into the bushes and trees again to await any unwanted surprises.

When the four alighted from the two horses and entered the gracious living room of the Harcourt mansion, Bert said, "Please try to forgive our rudeness when you arrived, but I didn't know who you were, and with the way things have been around here lately, I just didn't want to take any unnecessary chances."

Halleybelle nodded sadly. "Bert's right. You see, besides Grandma Harcourt's death and the problems around her passing, we seem to be at war!"

"With whom?" Jessie asked, looking from Halleybelle to Bert and back again.

Bert raised his shoulders helplessly. "That's just it—we don't know!"

"Then what do you mean?" Jessie asked. "How do you know you're at war? Are you being literal or figurative?"

"Literal," Bert said. "Believe me, there's nothing figurative or fictional about bullets."

"Obviously, you didn't attack anyone, or you'd know who it is. Who's fighting you?"

Halleybelle shrugged, her gingham gown crinkling audibly. "It's just as Bert said—we don't have any idea in the world who the enemy is. We just know that we've been shot at, one of our barns was torched, our cattle disappear without a trace—one at a time—someone poisoned our well, and when we go to town, something always happens to the buckboard on the way back." Her large brown eyes wide with anger, she snuffled gently. "Bert and I've been ambushed on the way home from town several times, two of our ranch hands have been shot. One died!"

Jessie said, "I'm sure you called in the law, didn't you? We saw the town marshal this morning. What does he think of all this?"

Bert replied bitterly, "That old buzzard all but called us liars and found a logical explanation for every single incident. Why, he even called Hector's death an accident—claimed the ranch hand shot himself while cleaning his own revolver."

Halleybelle said, "But, Jessica—Hector never owned a gun! He hated them. He worked for us tending the animals and working the kitchen garden. He didn't believe in violence, and he died violently. And the marshal will not believe us about Hector."

Ki rubbed his chin for a moment. "Perhaps there's a good reason for the marshal's reactions that the two of you may not yet have considered. Did it ever occur to you that the town marshal might be in on the war, on the other side—or the head of it?"

Both brother and sister gasped and looked at each other, nodding. Ki's words sounded right. And now the marshal's strange and baffling behavior made perfect sense. If Ki was right, and they had no reason to think not, they had been looking to the enemy for help.

As Halleybelle and Bert stared at Jessie and Ki in stunned silence, a rifle shot rang out and sent the four scrambling for cover.

★

Chapter 8

Jessica Starbuck and Ki dashed for the lights, blowing out the elaborate glass table lamps as they ran to the window. Halleybelle Harcourt crouched behind the ornate settee, while her brother reached for the Remington rifle he had replaced over the mantel. The shot from outside had burst through the big front window and then zinged through the immense living room, hitting no one but scattering everyone.

They all waited, poised and ready for more shots, but the only sounds to be heard came from the hounds out front raising a ruckus and frantic ranch hands racing back to the ranch house as fast as possible, their shouts and recriminations heard clearly from inside. Aside from barking, yelling and normal ranch sounds, everything seemed the same—no further rifle fire. The four inside the house looked at one another as the ranch hands hollered out and came barging through the front door, weapons ready.

"It's all right, boys," Bert Harcourt said calmly, "nobody's hurt here." He motioned to his men. "Caleb, Marty, Johnny—you go out and check all the way to the creek. Barney and Slim, you two get the rest of the boys and sweep around the other side of the house."

The ranch hands nodded and hurried out, ready to do battle. Barney stayed behind for a moment.

"Jeez, I'm sorry, boss," Barney said, his dark squinty eyes

51

full of worry. "Don't know how they got through us." His apologetic half-smile showed yellowed teeth. "I'm shore glad that nobody got hit!"

Bert glanced over at his sister, then at Jessica and Ki before answering. "Hey, we were lucky." He shook his head. "And there's no way you or the boys could protect us all the time. Just go get 'em now." Bert put his hand on Barney's broad shoulder. "You're the best foreman a rancher could have."

Barney slapped his sweat-stained ten-gallon hat on his leg and then crammed it down over his thinning black hair till his ears stuck out. He gave Halleybelle a quick smile and dashed out after Slim.

Ki said, "It would appear that whoever's been waging war against you sent Jessie and me a little warning. I'll stay here with the women if you want to get out there and hunt for the sniper with your men."

"Yes, Bert," Jessie added, "we'll be fine here. Go on before the sun disappears completely and you can't see anything."

As Bert raced out the door with his Remington rifle, Ki looked at Halleybelle and said, "I feel frustrated here, having to stay behind and protect you two. But Jessie and I don't know your ranch hands by sight, and some of them don't know us."

Jessie said, "That's right. Until we meet everyone, we could cause more harm than good out there." She chuckled. "Wouldn't want us to kill off some of your hired hands, now would you?"

Halleybelle smiled wanly and gazed out the window. "Of course not. I understand." She moved closer to the window to get a better view of her brother.

Ki jumped toward the shapely young Harcourt woman and pulled her from the window. "Keep away from there! I'm sorry if I hurt your arm, but standing in front of the window that way, you make an excellent target—even for someone who's retreating." He looked down at her large light brown eyes. "That sniper might not have been sending us a warning—he just might have been a bad shot. And there may have been more than one sniper out there."

Jessie drew the thick drapes from one side of the wide windows as Ki pulled from the other side. As soon as the heavily brocaded fabric blotted out the last of the sunlight, Halleybelle lighted a match and touched it to one of the table lamps' wicks and then the other. A yellowish glow filled the room with eerie shadows as flame flickered through the decorative glass shades. The three seated themselves tentatively on the settee and chairs. There would be no relaxing until Bert and the boys returned safely.

While they made small talk, all three strained to hear shots outside, hoping not to hear them.

Graham Greenleaf hopped off the train in Wichita, Kansas, his carpetbag much heavier than when he had left town months before. As he strutted down the boarded sidewalk from the train depot, lugging the weighty suitcase, he whistled a happy ditty and pondered his newfound wealth. Usually, after a good sales trip he arrived back in Wichita with few large bogus stock certificates to carry because he had sold most of them, and his carpetbag would be much lighter—but almost never completely empty—and his hard-earned money would be bulging in his pockets, crying out to be spent.

But this time, his swollen carpetbag weighed heftily with pounds and pounds of cash, and not one stock certificate left over to sell or even give away.

The dapper confidence man, trying not to look too conspicuous, crossed the rutted main street and strolled casually into an alleyway several blocks from the train station. He sauntered up to an unmarked side door that opened off into the alley, knocked hard three times and then gave two little soft taps before he pushed open the door and slipped through.

As his eyes grew accustomed to the darkness of the back room with its painted-over black windows, he called out in a low whisper: "Hey, Archie, you here? It's me, Greenie. I'm back."

"So what?" came a growl from the other side of the curtain in the next room.

"Aw, Archie, you aren't still mad at me, are yuh?" He strained to see, but little light penetrated the back room. "Well, if you're still holding a grudge, you won't be for long! Truth be told, I can hardly believe what happened to me myself!"

53

"Yeah? What?"

Graham Greenleaf, noticing that the man's tone had changed from complete indifference to mild interest, fairly bubbled with excitement. "I'm outta paper—plumb outta paper! Totally, entirely, completely out—sold out! Not one sheet left, not one scrap!"

The curtains parted, and the slender flimflam man could see a silhouette of a short man sporting a derby standing in the doorway. The little man reached up and turned on a gaslight, and a soft luminescence flooded both men in a glimmering glow as they stared at each other.

"Sold out?" Archie repeated, not quite certain whether the swindler might be joking or conning him.

"Every last piece, and I left the customers pleading for more! I don't know what happened. Truth be told, it's like I stumbled onto the motherlode." He laughed as he struggled to hold up his heavy carpetbag, then dropped it with a mighty thud onto the dirty wooden floor, sending dust flying and testing the old floorboards.

"I thought you said you was outta paper!" Archie spat, looking at the bulging bag.

The confidence man did a little dance around the colorful carpetbag and then bent over to open it. As his fingers pulled apart the clasps, he flung the bag open wide. "See! No more stock certificates!"

Archie's eyes sprang wide as he stared at the sight before him. "Jesus! I can't believe it!" The little man peered into the gaping carpetbag at the large gold coins and packets of greenbacks. "Gawd, Greenie, it's a real goddamn gold mine! Look at all that money!" He grabbed a handful of gold coins, running his fingers over the eight sides. "Jesus! Fifty-dollar gold pieces! We're rich!"

"You bet we are!" the confidence man crowed. "And after I pay you back what I owe you, I'm still gonna have tons of money to burn."

Greed played over Archie's features, changing his smile into a menacing leer. "What d'ya mean, pay me back what you owe me?" His voice turned vicious. "I thought we was partners on this—fifty-fifty."

54

Graham Greenleaf shook his head. "Hey, now, Archie . . . you staked me every time I went out, and you printed up the stock certificates . . . but you never said anything about us being fifty-fifty partners before."

Archie's fingers curled into tight fists, and his cheeks grew crimson, blazing around his light brown beard. Through clenched teeth, some of them missing, he said, "Well, I'm saying it now!"

"But I've never cheated you . . . I've always paid you double what you staked me, didn't I? And, truth be told, I always paid you much more for the certificates than the materials cost you." The slender swindler backed away, trying to calm the violence in Archie's eyes.

"Yeah, but it's hard work making all them certificates. It takes lots of time, and detailed artwork. Without them fancy stock certificates, you wouldn't have nuthin'!" The little man's tiny black eyes darted from the carpetbag to Graham Greenleaf and back, but the conversation had cost him some of his steam.

"Look, Archie, old buddy," Greenleaf said, as if speaking to a child, "I understand how you feel. After all, truth be told, you done such a good job on those shares of stock that folks'd flock to buy 'em. But this here's different." He backed away again, staying out of punching range. "This time, I practically had to fight the pigeons off. I mean, have I ever run out of stock certificates before?"

Archie grunted, raising his fists.

"Now, wait a minute, Archibald MacTaggert! There's no reason for us to fight." His swindler's smile beamed brighter than it had while he gathered up widows' savings. "There's enough here for both of us, and then some."

While Archie stood watching, Graham Greenleaf sat on a rickety chair next to the table in the middle of the room. He pushed aside a deck of cards and a hurricane lantern to make room for himself. From his inside breast pocket he pulled a large piece of paper with writing on one side. Turning it over, he stared at the blank page as he reached into his vest pocket for the nub of a pencil.

"What're you doin'?" Archie asked, his feet planted wide and his fists on his hips.

"Hold yer horses." The bony flimflam man licked the end of the pencil and made marks on the paper. Row after row of numbers, each row beneath the other. Finally, Greenleaf nodded and looked up.

"Well?" Archie demanded. "What's that all about? You tryin' to cheat me, you dirty diddler?"

"Nope. I'm just figuring out my expenses on the trip." He pointed at his numbers. "Archie, old buddy, I tell you what I'm gonna do . . . I'm gonna subtract my expenses and you're gonna take out your expenses. Then we're gonna split up the rest sixty-forty—that's sixty for me and forty for you."

"But—"

"Archie, be reasonable. Yes, you made the certificates, and without 'em I wouldn't have any money at all. But without my sales ability and"—he laughed—"my golden tongue, there wouldn't be any money."

"Oh, yeah?"

"Yeah! You've tried to sell 'em yourself. Remember what happened the last time you printed up extras and tried to sell them on your own?" Greenleaf looked pointedly at the little man's broken nose and missing earlobe. "Of course, truth be told, I think the face rearrangement was quite a great improvement, but I bet you anything you'd like to have those teeth back!"

"All right, so I ain't no great shakes at selling." Archie removed his derby long enough to scratch his balding head, then unbuttoned his sackcloth coat. "I guess there's enough there to take the sting outta life for a good long while . . . even split sixty-forty." He sat down at the table, on a chair opposite Graham Greenleaf, and pulled the paper out of the confidence man's hand. "Gimme yer pencil. I gotta figure out my expenses."

Greenleaf took off his dusty black traveling jacket, put the hook of the watch chain in the same pocket as his Waltham, and unbuttoned the matching vest. He leaned back and watched in fascination as Archie scribbled numbers down the side of the page. He already knew that the little man's expenses would add up to far more than his—to make up for the difference in the split—but it would be all right. If his sales charisma held up, the two of them would never have to worry about money again.

After the two men counted out their expenses and divvied up the rest of the money, there was far too much left over to carry on their person.

"Let's put most of it in the First National Bank of MacTaggert for safekeeping," Greenleaf said. "There's far too much to go carrying around with us." He grinned. "With the way my luck's been going, I doubt if we'll really need more, but if we should run out, we can always come back and get it."

"Good idea." Archie bent down and pried up several floor-boards, revealing a large rectangular hole in the earthen foundation under the flooring. "Yup, there's plenty of room down here." He looked up. "Greenie, grab those two metal boxes behind you."

Greenleaf handed Archie one of the boxes and kept the other. He brought out a pocketknife and pulled open the blade. "I'll scratch my initials on this box, and you cut yours into that one. That way, we won't get them mixed up," he said pointedly.

"Are you accusing me of—"

"No, Arch, I'm not accusing you of anything. I just want to make sure which one is which—for later." He carved as he talked. "After all, when we get low, we wouldn't want to get into the other's stash, now would we? I mean, it wouldn't be fair if I spent most of mine and then accidentally dipped into yours."

"Yeah, sure—accidentally . . . "

"Would you rather we put it all in one box and just dip into it as we need until it's all gone?"

"No thanks, Greenie, not the way you go through spondu-licks!" Archie took out a knife and scratched AMT on the top of his box.

Pockets filled with cash, the two men strolled out the front door of MacTaggart's Print & Sign Shop. After a brief stop at an expensive haberdasher for a new matching brown broad-cloth frock coat and vest to go with Graham Greenleaf's nan-keen trousers, the dapper swindler and his new partner headed quickly toward the Red Balloon Saloon and Gaming Hall—their reward for a confidence job well done.

★

Chapter 9

Although Bert and his ranch hands searched for well over an hour, they found nothing. One of the hounds had ripped into a shirt sleeve; Bert found the dog shaking a bloody piece of heavy handwoven cloth in his teeth. Darkness overtook them, and they reasoned that if the pattern held as with all the other attacks, they would fail to catch anyone. Bert called off the search and returned to the ranch house living room. Even with the massive drapes blanketing the windows, a chill had crept into the large room as the sun disappeared, and Ki and Halleybelle had put a log on. A blazing fire in the fireplace greeted Bert as he stepped through the front door and tossed his hat toward the hat rack.

Jessica Starbuck and Ki faced Bert Harcourt and his sister Halleybelle in the living room of the Circle H Ranch.

"It took more than an unknown enemy fighting you to force you to send us that telegram," Jessie said. "Am I right in assuming there's more?"

Bert and his sister nodded.

Ki jumped in. "You mentioned something about problems following your grandmother's death. Does it have anything to do with that?"

"Exactly!" Halleybelle said. "Of course, Granny Harcourt was well into her seventies and had had a good and full life. She died in her sleep with a smile on her face." A tear escaped the corner of her light brown eye and dribbled down her cheek. "That's Granny, up there with Grandpa Harcourt," she said, pointing to the large painting above the mantelpiece. "She was my favorite and raised Bert and me after our parents died."

Jessie and Ki waited patiently, understanding that the information would come in time.

Bert said, "Grandma Harcourt adored Halley." He smiled, his tanned nose crinkling. "Not that she didn't care for me, but little Halleybelle had always been everyone's darling, and especially Granny's."

A look of deep affection passed between Bert and his sister, a feeling of strong love that warmed Jessie and Ki more than the fire.

"Anyway," Bert continued, "when Grandma Harcourt died, we had a fine funeral with everyone in town attending, and friends coming from miles around. Everybody loved her and she cared for them—they were all dear to her heart."

Halleybelle nodded emphatically. "And when Lawyer Bledsoe read the will, she showed just how much she loved us all. She mentioned everybody in her will—leaving a little to this one and a little to that one—including something to Marshal Teddison."

"But," Bert jumped in, "naturally, she left the bulk of everything to us equally. Halley and I got all the property—this mansion and the ranch with all its cattle, and several other ranches and plots of land and buildings in town."

Jessie and Ki looked blankly at the brother and sister, waiting to hear the bad news.

Halleybelle's eyes teared up again. "And when we opened Granny's safe, we found thousands of shares of stock in the Henerow Corporation oil wells and mortgages on everything she owned."

Bert yelled, "Not a dime, not a penny—just mortgage papers!" The golden flecks in his light brown eyes all but danced with emotion. "We may own this mansion and the ranch and all the other properties, but if we can't come up with the mortgage payments, we lose everything!"

"And," Halleybelle said softly, "the Henerow stock is not worth the paper it was printed on. A flimflam man came through here some time back and sold everyone in Harcourt County his Oklahoma oil well stock, shares of stock in a Nebraska gold mine, and even stock in a bridge over the Mississippi!"

Jessica Starbuck smiled. "The money's no problem—I'll take care of your mortgage. But I think Ki and I should find that confidence man and get your money back for you . . . and for all the people around here."

Bert bristled. "There's no way I'll accept charity from anyone—especially from a woman!"

Halleybelle stared at her brother. "Bert! Jessie's our friend! She's not almsgiving, and you know it. It goes without saying that whatever money she provides would be a loan to keep the bank from foreclosing on us until we can get on a firm financial footing."

Jessie smiled. "I couldn't have said it better myself. If I spoke too offhandedly, Bert, I'm sorry. It's just that situations like this make my blood boil, and I just want to take charge and make things right."

"Yes, but—" Bert grumbled.

Halleybelle said, "Oh, hush! If you're worried about accepting money from a woman, just remember that Jessie's money comes from her father's fortune. Now would you have gotten all upset and turned down an offer of assistance from Alex Starbuck?"

"No . . . "

"Well, then, simply look at Jessie's offer as coming from her father's estate."

"Halley's right," Ki said, unable to hold his tongue a moment longer. "Jessie just jumped ahead of herself a little, but the plan is simple: One, we take care of the mortgage so you two aren't evicted. Two, we find that swindler and get your money back— if he hasn't already spent it all. And, three, we find out why the widow of the town's founder would have mortgaged everything she owned."

"Ki's right," Jessie said. "Something's wrong somewhere, above and beyond the swindler. But first things first."

Halleybelle laughed lightly. "Well, the first thing we should do is have supper." She looked out toward the kitchen and rang a brass bell by her chair.

A short, squat woman in her forties entered the room. "Yes, Miss Halleybelle? Supper is almost ready. You may come to the table now, if you wish, but I would imagine your guests would like to clean up first."

"Thank you, Angelita." Halley smiled at Jessie. "If I remember, yours was named Marguerita?"

Jessie shook her head. "What a memory! Yes, and she's still with us." When the housekeeper had left the room, Jessie said, "Angelita has blue eyes, I notice, and speaks excellent English."

"Her father was a friend of our father's from England," Bert said, "and her mother was Mexican and Choctaw. An exotic combination, don't you think?"

Halleybelle smiled softly. "Besides Granny, Angelita was like a mother to me. She was married to Hector, God rest his soul. I'll have Angelita get your things off your horses while we're eating. But I'll take you to your rooms now so you can wash up."

In less than fifteen minutes, Ki and Jessie returned to the living room, both looking a lot fresher. As they headed for the dining room and a festive dinner, Jessie said, "Now, tell Ki and me what that flimflam man looked like. We'll probably take off after him tomorrow or the next day, but we can't give him too much time."

"If only we had a picture," Halleybelle lamented as Ki pulled her chair out for her. "Bert and I went to town and asked the marshal if we could look through all the wanted posters, but no luck. Of course, both of us met the crook only once, and then for just a few seconds."

"Yes," Bert shot in as he seated Jessica, "if only we had known then what we know now—"

Jessie smiled sadly. "Hindsight is wonderful. So you both met him, did you?" She undid her napkin and slid it across her lap. "That's good news. A description is better than nothing."

"Grandma Harcourt introduced him to each of us, so we know his name," Bert said. "He's Graydon Greenfield or Graystone Greenley or Graham Greenbaum—something like that. I can't remember."

"No," Halleybelle said, "it was Gregory Greenwood. I remember thinking what a lovely name it was. But I was in and out of the house in moments, and didn't really pay much attention to his appearance—except for his soft hands."

While the four discussed the swindler, Angelita brought steaming bowls of food to the table. After placing the last of the inviting victuals on hot pads, she said, "Excuse me, Miss Halley, but the man's name was Graham Greenleaf." She proceeded to give Jessie and Ki a complete and comprehensive description of the confidence man and his possible destination.

Everyone enjoyed a hearty meal, with Bert eyeing Jessie and Halley intrigued with Ki. In a day or two, the adventurous Lone Star duo would be off for Oklahoma City to capture the crook and return the stolen money. But in the meantime, there seemed no reason why they should not share some pleasurable moments together.

After large brandies, the Harcourts showed their guests to their rooms. In the room next to Halleybelle's, Jessica found an intimate fire glowing in the fireplace and a bed warmer at the foot of the huge canopy bed. Ki's room, across the hall and next to Bert's, had also been visited by Angelita. Both Jessie and Ki looked forward to a good night's sleep.

Jessie undressed quickly, anticipating her first night in a bed in several days. She slipped between the satiny covers and stretched luxuriously. How delicious, she thought, not to have to wear her clothes to bed. She always felt constricted, even in a flowing nightgown. Naked skin against expensive material teased her sense of touch. Her warm flesh quivered with pleasure as she felt the smoothness and delicate softness of the sheets covering her. As she settled her head on the down pillow, she thought she heard a slight noise at the door. Yes, there it was again. She became immediately awake and alert.

By the light of dying embers in the fireplace, she saw the door handle twist. She froze and waited, prepared for an attack. Of course, if she cried out, Ki and Bert were right across the hall. But a lot could happen between a cry for help and a dash across the hall—assuming someone heard her through the thick oak door and walnut wall paneling. She slid her hand out from under the covers until her fingers wrapped securely around the cool steel of her six-shooter on the nightstand.

The door swung open a crack, and Jessie inched the Colt revolver toward her and muffled it under the covers before cocking it. The intruder stopped, obviously having heard the *click* of a gun. Jessie strained to see who had entered and saw a large menacing shadow moving toward her from the doorway.

★

Chapter 10

Jessica Starbuck edged the .45 Colt revolver from under the bed covers where she had just cocked it. She pointed it in the direction of the shadowy figure that had moments before invaded her bedroom in the Harcourt mansion and waited. A worm in the smoldering remnants of a log in the fireplace popped with a loud crackle, and both she and the intruder jumped.

"Jessie?" a deep whisper called out. "Are you asleep yet?"

Jessie sat up. "Bert! For crissake, I could have shot you!"

The handsome Harcourt heir moved into the light and grinned sheepishly. "That's why I called out. I heard you cock your revolver, and I saw you jump."

She shook her head. "That was a close call. You really like to live dangerously, don't you?"

Bert Harcourt shrugged off his monogrammed satin lounging robe and approached the bed, his rugged naked body silhouetted against the shining embers. "Sorry, Jess . . . I didn't mean to scare you. I just wanted to kiss you awake, that's all. I've missed you so much, and I simply couldn't wait to get my hands on you."

"That's very romantic, but how romantic would it have been had I shot you dead?" She placed the six-shooter back on the night table and reached up her arms to him. "I missed you, too," she said, grabbing his firm buttocks and pulling him down to her.

She delighted in the sight of his bobbing erection and kissed the tip as the delicious scent of masculinity all but overpowered her. She inhaled deeply as Bert dropped to his knees beside the bed and sank his hands into her long honey-blond tresses, lifting her head toward his hungry mouth. His lips touched hers tentatively, and his tongue teased her lips with the heat of desire. She opened her mouth instinctively, inviting him in, and their tongues entwined, each enticing the other as their sensuous kiss built in intensity, stimulating their juices.

Jessie pushed back the covers, and Bert slipped into bed alongside her, his solid flesh caressing hers. As they kissed harder and more passionately, they rolled over, taking advantage of the entire bed. Legs entangled, arms wrapped tightly around each other, they reveled in the sexual excitement of their kisses.

As they rolled over again, Bert pulled back and cradled Jessie's breasts in his hands. Rigid nipples, suddenly brought fiercely erect, pressed urgently against his palms, crying out for more. He tore at her breasts as she writhed in sweet desire, his erection pushing into her magnificent thigh. She yelled out with pleasure, and he bent to kiss her breast, his tongue taunting her engorged nipple. Her hips thrust forward, eagerly pounding his upper leg with her silky moistness.

Bert got up on one knee to straddle her writhing body, but she pulled him to her, crushing her aching nipples into his chest and encircling his body with her legs. They kissed hard, their moist flesh straining to blend. Suddenly, Jessie rolled Bert over and came up on top. She sat back on her haunches and caressed his rippling stomach muscles, her soft fingers stroking his tense little nipples, his inward navel. Then, toying with his massive shaft, she kissed his eyelids, nibbled on the tip of his nose, and bit seductively into his cheeks.

Jessie's lips and tongue traced circles across Bert's chest, and she nipped affectionately at his nipples until his rampant shaft beat a rapid tattoo against her tummy. She moaned with pleasure as her lips nibbled along his chest hairs, trailing down to his belly. His eyes closed, Bert grabbed Jessie's silken hair and held her head to his body, straining for whatever exotic delight might follow.

66

She lifted herself up, carefully positioning her hips directly above his, and enveloped his erection within her, sliding down until her moist warmth took in every inch of him. He groaned as she wriggled her hips and reached back for his huge sac. His yelp of pleasure stimulated her more, and she ground herself into him.

Bert's hands grasped her flawless breasts, and he stroked them as she gracefully swayed and pitched on his shaft as if riding an unbroken bronc. The rhythm of her movements grew in intensity as she picked up the pace. Suddenly, she threw her head back, her magnificent breasts jutting forward, and a low moan seemed to come up from deep within her. Bert slid his fingers between her legs, and his thumb massaged her swollen, pulsating nub of pleasure. Her body shook, and her moistness clamped down on his erection and squeezed it repeatedly as a throaty cry escaped her lips.

"Oh, yes, Bert. Oh, my God, that's so good—that's *it*!" Her hips swiveled as she smashed herself against him, grinding faster and faster.

Bert quickly pulled Jessie to him, kissing her fully as his aching loins thrust into her deeper and deeper. He bit into her lips and clasped her face in his hands tightly. Then he rolled her over onto her back and ground himself into her as she moaned with delight. He rocked and bucked, shoving himself farther into her depths, as his mouth surrounded her breast.

"Oh, yes!" Jessie cried. "Oh, Bert, yes!"

Her words served to stimulate him more, and he thrust even faster into her. His pace quickened, and, glistening with perspiration, he smothered Jessie's glowing face with kisses as he felt a sudden powerful release. Shuddering, he relaxed, still on top of her, his hips and pelvis slowing to a stop.

Finally, the first heat of passion assuaged, Bert and Jessie lay in each other's arms and slept more deeply than either had in a very long time. As a rooster announced the approach of daybreak, the two awakened just enough to realize they were still together, cuddled comfortably in each other's arms. They both enjoyed the warmth of the other's presence and sighed contentedly.

Softly, gently, without the burning hunger and frantic passion of the night before, they stroked each other and kissed tenderly. This time, when Jessie's tongue and lips made magical inroads on Bert's chest and belly, he reciprocated. Leisurely, lovingly, they gave each other affectionate pleasure and satisfaction. They purposely prolonged the inevitable conclusion, reveling in giving each other more and more ecstasy.

When the morning sun's bright rays spilled in through the windows, only partially blocked by the chintz curtains, they lay back in each other's arms and sighed. Bert kissed Jessie one last time on the nose and eyelids and slipped reluctantly from her bed.

He stood looking down at her, the gold specks in his light brown eyes flashing with admiration. "God, you're delicious!"

Bert's manhood sprang to life again, and he leaned over to kiss Jessie, his hands groping for her perfect breasts, teasing the huge nipples taut once more.

"My little tigress," he whispered.

She reached up to pull his neck down, but instead, she thought better of it and pushed him away.

"We'll have more time later, but right now we have too much to do and time is short." Her large green eyes pleaded with him to stay, but her arms held him back.

"You're right." He smiled and kissed each nipple. "We have a lot of tomorrows ahead of us." Bert picked up the robe he had dropped the night before and quickly crossed the hallway to his room.

Jessie watched him leave, a warm fuzzy feeling in her groin. Then her glance fell on the six-shooter on the nightstand, and reality flooded back as once again she remembered her original mission.

★
Chapter 11

People stared as Jessica Starbuck and Ki dismounted in front of the Bank of Harcourtville. Purple was one of Jessie's best colors, because it accentuated the lusciousness of her honey-blond tresses, and the low-cut silky purple blouse she wore showed off her bust to best advantage. Her tight gray jeans hugged the outline of her buttocks, cutting into the rear, firing men's imaginations and flaming women's indignation. Pubescent girls noted that the blonde's gray leather boots matched her jeans and tiny leather vest. Pubescent boys had difficulty covering their growing interest.

Again, few people took any notice of the tall Japanese-American in his black jeans and loose cotton shirt. Some looked with curiosity at his headband or his moccasins, but almost everyone concentrated on Jessie.

Inside the bank, customers and tellers stopped speaking as Jessie and Ki entered. They're looking at us as if we're about to rob the bank! Jessie thought as she headed for the bank president's office. Purposely keeping her hand as far from her six-shooter as possible, she approached the young clerk whose desk fronted the office. She leaned over the counter and smiled, her bosom displayed by the cut of the blouse for his eyes only.

"Miss Starbuck and associate to see the bank president. We

sent word this morning that we'd be in," she said softly, her green eyes never wavering.

The clean-shaven, young bank clerk gulped and tried to keep his eyes from straying below Jessie's face, but the more he tried, the redder his face became. He turned and knocked on the bank officer's door, announcing the two strangers. Making a valiant attempt to remain calm, he returned to the counter and said, "Blister Medsoe will see you now . . . I mean, *Mr. Bledsoe*—"

Jessie and Ki swept past the young man. "Thank you very much," she whispered as she walked by.

"Hiram, ma'am, Hiram Abernathy at your service . . . any time."

Jessie turned and smiled briefly before following Ki into an extremely ornate office. The gigantic, dark, well-polished mahogany desk all but filled the room. On its top, an expensive table lamp with a colored glass shade and a large ceramic ashtray blended maroons and grays and blues. In a prominent position, facing guests, was a recent issue of the *New York Times*. Back issues on a side table near the massive leather chesterfield suggested the bank had a subscription.

Elegant touch, Jessie thought as she inspected the bank president's office in one sweeping appraisal. Ki's raised eyebrow confirmed her first impression.

A tall, well-built gentleman who appeared to be in his late sixties greeted them. His attire suggested social prominence and financial security—a three-piece suit of the finest cloth, probably from England, Jessie reflected. His cravat added a touch of color and daring—bright crimson against a charcoal gray suit. The diamond stickpin could only be real, its facets dazzling.

"Miss Starbuck and Mr. Ki . . . by gum, what a pleasure to make your acquaintance." The bank president extended his hand to each. "I am Maxwell Bledsoe, the Harcourt's attorney and president of the Bank of Harcourtville. How may I help you?" The large man smiled broadly and stroked his magnificent silvery muttonchops. "Are you planning to deposit some of the legendary Lone Star fortune here? Or am I presuming too much?"

Jessie sat in one of the soft leather chairs in front of Bledsoe's desk and smiled. "So you've heard of us. Then you must know my associate and I are here to find out what happened to the Harcourt fortune. From what Bert and Halleybelle tell us, their grandmother mortgaged everything she owned just before she died."

Bledsoe sank into the oversized deep maroon leather chair behind his desk, motioning for Ki to take a seat. "Yes, this is so," he said stiffly. Then his voice softened, and he reached for one of the many decorative pipes on a rack behind his desk. "Esmeralda Harcourt, God rest her generous soul, thought only of her grandchildren. I'm sure you know she all but raised Bert Junior and Halleybelle singlehanded."

Jessie and Ki nodded and waited.

He struck a match and lighted the coarse tobacco shreds in the bowl of his pipe, puffing heavily until the flame took hold. "She wanted to assure their financial security, don't y'know. Sadly, a common swindler gained her confidence and sold her worthless shares of oil stock."

"But why," Ki asked, "would she mortgage everything to buy stock? Didn't she have cash and liquid assets at her disposal?"

Jessie added, "Yes, after all, she was the widow of the founder of this town and one of the wealthiest men this side of the Mississippi. What happened? She had money, didn't she?"

Bledsoe shook his head. "Of course she did. But that flimflam man turned this county upside-down, don't y'know. He had everyone convinced that oil had just been struck in Wetumka—a town east of here—and that the people around these parts could get in on the ground floor of what would turn into a financial boom like no one ever saw before." He scratched his silvery whiskers and puffed at his pipe, blue circles of smoke wafting toward the ceiling. "He created such a furor in the county, by gum, that even I bought some of his stock! I who pride myself on never being taken!"

Jessie nodded sympathetically. "But as her lawyer and president of the bank, couldn't you have talked Mrs. Harcourt out of mortgaging everything she owned?"

The bank president shook his head sadly. "Miss Starbuck, Esmeralda Harcourt wasn't the only one who insisted on mortgaging property. I handled several transactions a day. It was akin to a run on the bank. I think it started with the Hodgsons out to the west of here. Yes, young Daniel Hodgson asked me to personally lend him money against his cattle ranch. When I turned him down because his herd is small and his ranch was just getting started, he asked the bank to mortgage his property."

"Didn't he tell you why he needed so much cash?" Jessie asked.

"Not at first. He seemed most insistent, said that if we gave him the money, he could get in on something that would set him up for life. He said he could retire before he turned thirty-five." Bledsoe tapped the pipe's ashes into a large Limoges ashtray and blew into the stem. "The bank officers agreed quickly enough—Hodgson's piece of land is well situated, don't y'know. They reasoned that the bank couldn't lose. If the oil shares proved as good an investment as Daniel thought, he'd be in a position to pay us back with interest." He pulled at his whiskers and smiled. "On the other hand, if the bottom fell out of everything, the Hodgson property was well worth investing in. Either way, they figured, the bank would come out a winner."

"What made everyone think the oil stock was such a good buy?" Ki asked.

Maxwell Bledsoe ruffled his muttonchops while he thought. "By gum, I don't rightly know. Everything happened so fast—it seemed like such a good idea at the time, don't y'know. We were all acting quite foolish. Greed sometimes makes people do strange things."

"Well, Ki and I plan to catch up with the rogue and see if we can't get everyone's money back."

"By gum, that would be splendid!"

"By the way," Jessie added as she rose to leave, "the Harcourts are having trouble remembering the swindler's name. If you bought stock from him, you must know his name, and perhaps even a little about him?"

"More's the pity, but I do. The scalawag's name is Graham Greenleaf—at least, that's the name he gave me—and he claims to be from St. Louis by way of Oklahoma City, or so he said." Bledsoe filled his pipe with shreds of spicy-smelling tobacco.

"He works . . . I should say, he *claimed* to work for the Henerow Corporation, an international cartel with headquarters in New York City and branch headquarters in Oklahoma City."

"Didn't you or anyone else think to wire Oklahoma City to verify the corporation's existence?" Jessie asked, her hand on the doorknob.

The bank president cleared his throat and coughed regally, his face flushing. "By gum, I did send a letter of enquiry. And I received a formal letter on such handsome stationery that I immediately believed in the Henerow Corporation." He pulled open a drawer and riffled through the papers. "I have it here somewhere . . . "

The bank president went through one drawer after another as Jessica pulled open the door. Ki held the door as she started out.

Jessie said, "We'll keep in touch, Mr. Bledsoe. Thank you very much for your cooperation. You've been most helpful."

"How do you do, Marshal Teddison. My name is Jessica Starbuck, and this is my associate Ki."

Harcourtville's town marshal took his time responding to the honey-blonde, his eyes lingering on her jutting, unencumbered breasts, her narrow waist and her voluptuous hips before meeting her huge light green eyes. Instead of standing to greet her, he pointedly pushed his wooden chair back onto two legs and propped his scuffed leather boots up atop the paperwork on his desk. He chomped down on a long, crooked, unlit stogie and swallowed some of the juice before spitting into a nearby spittoon. Two tough-looking deputies lounged on either side of him; the big blond with a scraggly attempt at a beard twirled a six-shooter on his index finger while the acne-faced younger fellow picked at a pimple and openly admired Jessie's feminine attributes.

"Howdy," the marshal said, "and welcome to Harcourtville." His gaze switched to Ki as he stared at the *te* master's long black hair, weaponless belt and soft moccasins. "Ki, huh? You're pretty good with your hands 'n' feet, ain't yuh, Chinaman?"

"Thank you, but I am Japanese-American."

Jessie said, "We're here to find out about the confidence man who passed through town a short time ago. Halleybelle Harcourt tells us none of the wanted posters look like the man. Mr. Bledsoe says his name is Graham Greenleaf of Oklahoma City."

The lawman leered. "Hear there was some trouble out at the Circle H yesterday. You two shore bring a heap of bad news with you, don't yuh?"

"We don't look for it," Ki said, "but we don't run away from it when it comes our way. Right now, we're planning on finding that flimflam man and getting the Harcourts back their money."

"By what authority?" Marshal Teddison growled.

Jessie smiled. "What authority do we need, Marshal? Two close friends have asked my associate and me to look into the matter and see if it's possible to get back their late grandmother's money." She looked at the deputies and then at the grizzled marshal's balding spot on the top of his head. "Do you have a problem with that . . . Marshal?"

The marshal's eyes closed as he looked at Jessica and Ki through the merest of slits. His teeth ground into the stogie as he chewed on the slippery tobacco. "Nope, but I don't care much for people wandering into town and causing a rumpus." For emphasis, he spat into the spittoon, splattering the side of the desk. "To tell you the truth, ma'am, I ain't got much use for women that dress like men and act like men but expect to be treated like ladies." His eyes dropped to the six-shooter at Jessie's side.

Ki's jaw grew firm, and he took a step forward. "Miss Starbuck is more of—"

Jessie grabbed hold of Ki's shoulder. "Marshal, I have asked no favors, and I expect no special treatment. And while I would prefer the same courtesy you might extend to any other stranger to town who's willing to go out of his way to help Harcourtville's citizens, Ki and I can get along without it." She tightened the drawstring under her chin, securing her flat-crowned hat, and adjusted her holster. "I'm sorry to have taken up so much of your valuable time. Ki and I will conduct our own investigation and will stay well out of your way." She smirked. "Wouldn't want to get on the wrong side of the law, now would we?"

Before the lawmen could respond, Jessie and Ki left the jailhouse and led their horses across the street to the hitching rail in front of Mom's Grub Shop. As they climbed the steps, they could see that the breakfast crowd had thinned out.

"Well, now, look who's here!" a cheery voice called out from the back of the little restaurant. "If it isn't Beauty and the Best!"

Ki chuckled, pleased with Mike's complimentary pun, and nodded at the Irish chef. "Hello there, Mike. Good to see you again."

Jessie laughed. "Good morning, Mike. How's the coffee?" She glanced over at the counter, where three respectable-looking men stared at her purple blouse and its contents. "How's the coffee cake?" she asked. "It looks good. We've already had breakfast, so that and some coffee is about all we need."

The pair took the same table they had had the day before, and Mike hurried to fill their order.

Mike's sky blue eyes gleamed, and his orange mustache fairly twitched with pleasure, as he approached the table with his arms loaded, balancing the pastry plates on the front of his dirty apron. "That was some show you two put on out there yesterday! Handy bit o' footwork, Ki. You surely taught those two hooligans a lesson they sorely needed. Big bullies, the both of 'em." He stepped back as he placed the steaming mugs and fresh baked goods on the table. "Those two yahoos didn't happen to give you no trouble last night, now did they?"

As Jessie sipped her coffee, Ki said casually, "Why do you ask?"

"Well, sir, I heard them talkin' after you left. They said somethin' about fixin' yer wagon—and you ain't got no wagon." He laughed at his pun. "So I figure them two bullies meant they was gonna try to pay you back for the lickin' you give 'em."

"As a matter of fact," Jessie said after she washed down a bite of coffee cake with coffee, "someone did snipe at us just after we arrived at the Harcourt ranch."

75

"Was anyone hurt?" Mike demanded.

"No, a clean miss," Ki said. "But someone shot at us through the Harcourt mansion living-room window. We thought the sniper was out to get the Harcourts." He looked at Jessie. "It never occurred to us that Jessie or I might have been the target."

"And if it hadn't been for Bert's hounds, they might have bagged their target!" Jessie added. "Mike, what do you know of a confidence man named Graham Greenleaf?"

The round little man did a bit of a jig and made a sour face. "That smooth-talkin' humbug of a fraud tried to sell me shares in a phony oil company. I laughed him off and told him where he could go with his bleedin' scheme." He winked. "No one pulls the wool over the eyes of Michael O'Murray!" He beamed proudly. "O' course, I couldn't get Esmeralda Harcourt to listen to me. I think she bought a few shares, and so did the Hodgsons and the Creightons and the Baumgartners." He smiled wanly. "But who listens to a cook right off the boat from Ireland— surely not the folks of Harcourtville."

Jessie shook her head. "Too bad you didn't make more noise. That swindler took nearly everyone in the county for a great deal of money. Ki and I are going to track him down and get it back for them."

Mike's face ruddied as his eyes grew almost red. "If there's anything I can do to help, me friends, just you holler 'n' Michael O'Murray'll be there in half the time it takes to do a jig."

After stopping off at the Circle H Ranch to fill Bert and Halleybelle in on what they had found out, Jessie and Ki made two additional stops before hitting the trail for Oklahoma City. They stopped at a ranch to the east of town and spoke with the Baumgartners. Clarence and Ermogene Baumgartner had been fleeced of all their cash and had mortgaged their home and their farm. With pressure from the bank and no cash to pay their mortgage payments, the couple and their eleven offspring felt desperate. They were about to be evicted from the land they had worked for so long.

Clarence Baumgartner had traveled out West from upper New York State, hoping to find the ideal place to raise a family in peace and security. His parents had come from the Old Country and had struggled for every penny and every piece of food.

Clarence knew that if he could have some land of his own, he could be self-sufficient. He came out to the territory beyond Arkansas and Kansas and settled on a fertile spread near a creek. After he built a small cabin and worked the soil for a while, he sent for his childhood sweetheart, Ermogene, and started a family.

The Baumgartners' happiness with each new offspring and the burgeoning farmland had seemed complete. They had planned to stop bearing children when they reached an even dozen, so that Ermogene could relax and have only the chores to tend to. The children took care of themselves—the eldest raising the third and fourth, the next oldest raising the fifth and sixth, and so on.

When Graham Greenleaf approached the Baumgartners with his offer to make their wildest dreams come true, they felt that it must be right, since everything else out West had gone so well for them up until then. And with the extra money from their shares in an oil gusher, they could buy all the latest farm implements, hire some extra hands, and double their crop in a year.

They never noticed when their joy turned to greed, not until it was too late and they had squandered their complete life savings and everything they had worked so hard for. Jessie and Ki sadly listened to their story, which sounded very much like those of the other families they had spoken with.

After spending more time than they had anticipated at the Baumgartner place, Jessie and Ki stopped off at the nearest stagecoach station and sent a telegram to Oklahoma City. They were assured that the information they requested would be forwarded to Enid, their next stop on the trail of the confidence man.

★
Chapter 12

Jessica Starbuck sat high in the saddle astride her palomino mare, savoring the memory of the previous night with Bert Harcourt. His musky scent stayed in her nostrils, haunting her, distracting her. She knew she should concentrate on the problem at hand, but her thoughts kept boomeranging back to the delicious hours of pleasure in Bert's arms.

Ki rode his sorrel gelding in silence, playing over in his mind what had happened at the Baumgartner farm. How could anyone with a wife and eleven children mortgage everything to buy stock in an unknown, untried oil company? It made no sense, and the bank's permitting the mortgage to go through made even less sense. Yes, the bank had been swamped with requests—no, demands—for mortgages, but in all good conscience, how could Maxwell Bledsoe allow a man with twelve people depending on him for survival to risk losing the farm? Oil shares had always been a gamble, and it appeared strange that a solid citizen with so much to lose would take such a flier.

Ki mulled the puzzle over in his mind, thinking it through one way, then switching it around to look at it from a different point of view. But no matter how he wrestled with it, he always came to the same conclusion: Something was very wrong somewhere. That Graham Greenleaf must be quite some sweet-talker! Ki mused.

A breeze came up from the southwest, blowing hot wind and rolling tumbleweeds across their path. Extremely high cumulus clouds stayed at the riders' backs, but the heavier the clouds grew, the faster they seemed to approach. The sun ducked behind a small patch of clouds, drenching the plains in dark gray shadows.

"Looks like we might be in for some weather," Ki said, breaking the long silence.

Jessie glanced up, twisting in her saddle to see off to the west. "You're right." She prodded her mare with her heels. "Let's pick it up so we can get some distance in before the storm hits. From the looks of it, I doubt that we can outrun it, but let's make some time now while we still can."

With a sharp slap of the reins, both horses took off at a powerful gallop, heading away from the oncoming storm. Jessie and Ki stayed to the trail, heading straight east, away from the storm. The sky ahead looked clear and blue, but each time clouds blanketed the sun, the eastern horizon grew vague. A brightening of the sky around them announced the flash of lightning behind them, followed many seconds afterward by the distant rumble of thunder. But as the wind picked up, the delay between lightning flashes and thunder crashes became shorter and shorter.

Jessie and Ki leaned as far over their horses as possible and fairly flew through the sagebrush of the Indian Territory plains. They gave no thought to the possibility of another Comanche raid, because any warriors out there would be in the same danger from nature's wrath as they were. They knew that with summer storms came lightning strikes and dangerous flash floods, and they needed to get to high ground and the safety of cover before the storm clouds overtook them and put them in complete jeopardy.

Off to the southeast, they could see a bluff thrusting sky-ward—a place of high ground where flash floods would not be a danger. Caves in the rock formation would afford them shelter from the lightning and the driving rain. They headed toward the bluff, trying to get to the other side of the dry riverbed before the rains swelled its banks and drowned every living thing in its path. Jessie's palomino stumbled but righted itself.

Ki slowed to make sure Jessie and her mare were all right.

As they reduced their pace for the moment, what sounded like a very loud clap of thunder rang out and echoed much too close. But there had been no lightning, and the noise seemed to have come from the east. Ki headed his sorrel for a clump of dusty trees, calling for Jessie to follow. As he grabbed his rifle and jumped from his horse, she did the same. Throwing the reins around a low branch, they dove for cover.

"That wasn't thunder!" Ki called out.

"I know!" Jessie said. "There's a hole in the brim of my hat!"

They flattened themselves beside the trees and searched the brush up ahead for movement. Ki leaned over to get a better look at the hole in Jessie's hat. "We're lucky someone got overeager. Otherwise, we'd have ridden right into an ambush, and we'd both be dead now."

Jessie nodded as she put the hat back on her head and pulled the chin strap tight.

Another shot rang out, ripping a hunk of bark off the tree trunk just above their heads. The sky to the west became dark, then lighted up the entire area. Thunder rippled through the air, and several more shots pelted the trees and ground where they lay—all from a clump of bushes on either side of the gully they had planned to head through on the way to the bluff. Ki counted four rifles firing, two from one side and two from the other.

He said, "You take the ones on the right, and I'll get the ones on the left."

Hidden by the high sagebrush, Ki crawled off well to the left as Jessie gave him fire cover. She shot into the bushes on one side and then the other, keeping the bushwackers busy as he skittered along, his Winchester cradled in his arms. The thunder claps grew louder, and the lightning flashes brighter and more frequent; the storm approached relentlessly, the winds building in intensity and the pungent odor of ozone hanging in the air as a warning.

Jessie took sight, adjusting her aim for the wind and the distance. On the next lightning flash, she squeezed the trigger, and from somewhere within the bushes, a scream of agony followed on the heels of a violent roll of thunder. As the darkened sky lighted up like millions of candles again, one of the bushwackers half-stood and shot off his rifle into the air several times as he collapsed back into the bushes.

Bullets sang by Jessie, and she rolled over to change positions. She buried several rounds into the clump of sagebrush where the first bushwacker fell. Shots came from a bush a few feet away. She sighted on the new location and peppered the area. That gun fell silent for the moment, while the other two delivered a constant barrage her way.

"When's Ki gonna get there?" she muttered, reloading her Winchester.

Ki had swung himself around so that he could sneak up on the bushwackers from behind. As the sky lighted up brighter than noon, and deafening thunder crashed overhead, Ki saw his quarry. Indians! From the look of them—the war paint and attire—Kiowa. The martial-arts master didn't wait to find out why four lone Kiowa braves would be attacking them from ambush or why they weren't on horseback during the attack. Rather than call attention to his position, he put his Winchester aside and reached into his vest pocket for a smooth, cold *shuriken*. With deadly aim, he pinpointed the warrior closest to him and spun the throwing star toward its target.

To go for the throat was out of the question, since the brave's long hair covered both neck and shoulders. Ki estimated trajectory and let fly, aiming at the spine. With astonishing accuracy, he propelled the death star into the painted warrior's back. The bushwacker slumped forward without making a sound, his body falling limp. The two remaining bushwackers, one on either side of the gully, exchanged quick rifle fire with Jessie, who took turns shooting at one and then the other as she bided time until Ki was ready to strike from behind.

Ki dipped his fingers into the vest pocket for another *shuriken*, but before he could withdraw it, the partner of the bushwacker he had just killed looked back at his friend and saw him lying face-down with a metal star jutting from the middle of his back. Ki, realizing he was about to be spotted, went immediately on the offensive. In three powerful strides, he crossed the distance between them and, hands outstretched, dove at the painted brave.

As the bushwacker rolled over and tried to aim his Remington at Ki, a shot pierced the air, knocking the rifle from the warrior's hands. The rifle spun off to the side, its stock splintered by one of Jessie's better shots. Her sharpshooting continued as she traded shots with the Kiowa on the other side of the gully. She finally had his range and narrowed in for the kill, each rifle blast getting closer than the one before. At the moment when a forked bolt of lightning touched down in three sites nearby and a thunder clap sounded directly overhead, the pinned-down Kiowa brave made a run for his steed. Clinging to the side of his horse, he galloped off to the southwest.

Ki sprang toward the disarmed warrior, kicking at his chin. But the Kiowa brave caught Ki by surprise and grabbed the tall Japanese-American's foot with both hands, twisting it viciously. The stunned *te* master went sprawling, landing hard on his right hip. As the bushwacker came at him with knife raised, Ki leaped to his feet as quick as a panther and blocked the oncoming blade with a *gedan-barai* by crossing his wrists and turning the painted warrior's blow aside as he turned his body.

The bushwacker's forward motion kept him going, and he tripped on a batch of sagebrush. He staggered a step or two, trying to right himself, but Ki had the advantage he needed and delivered a deadly *teri-gobi* kick to the back. The Kiowa died before his body hit the ground.

Off beneath the trees, Jessica heard a loud *oof* and the snap of what sounded like a bone breaking and knew instinctively that Ki had prevailed. She pulled herself up and peeked over the sagebrush, using the trunk of the tree as protection. By the grayish light of the storm, she saw Ki's silhouette on the ridge above the gully to her left.

Ki looked around. No further shots sounded, and all remained still but the rumble of thunder and crackle of lightning passing overhead. Gigantic drops of rain stung him one at a time as he headed toward the other side of the gully to see if all the bushwackers were dead.

Jessie called out to him, "One got away." She gathered up Ki's horse with hers and made her way to where Ki stood searching for something.

"And three are dead," Ki said. He covered his brow with his

hand to keep the rain from hitting him squarely in the eyes as he tried to see through the storm's feeble light. The midafternoon sun hid behind the clouds, and visibility was short.

Jessie handed Ki the reins to his gelding and mounted her mare. "Let's get out of here before we're caught by a flash flood."

"Fine," Ki said, "but something's bothering me here—something just isn't right."

"What? Any idea?"

"No, just a feeling." Ki gazed off into the distance. "I wish the clouds would lift so I could see better. It's right on the edge of my mind, but I can't quite grab hold of it."

"Do you want to stay here until it comes to you, or can we move on?" Jessie asked, respecting his instincts and intuition.

As Ki made a decision to let it go and ride off, one of the bushwacker's horses wandered up, nudging a succulent piece of prairie grass with its tongue. The rope bridle in its mouth made it difficult for the animal to eat.

"That's it!" Ki yelled, bounding over to the nearest dead body. He bent over and took the brave's mass of black hair in his hand and pulled—and yanked it completely off the man's head.

Jessie gasped. "That's the neatest scalping I ever saw!" She stared at the head of hair under the long black hair in Ki's hand.

"This fellow's not an Indian!" he said, holding up the wig and headband. Ki stalked over to the bushwacker with the *shuriken* buried in his back and ripped the wig off that body, too. He threw it back down in disgust. "They tried to make us think they were Kiowa renegades, just in case one of us lived and got away."

Jessie's face grew somber, and her green eyes turned dark and sad. "That means this was no random ambushing war party. These killers were out after us and meant to stop us in our tracks."

"And very nearly would have if one of them hadn't gotten a mite too eager and shot too soon." He looked up into the raindrops. "I think the impending storm spooked one of 'em.

84

I bet they hadn't counted on a storm coming up like this. He probably wanted to get the ambush over with quickly so he could get out of here before the rain came." Ki swung himself up on his horse quickly. "Which is what we had better do right now."

Together, Ki and Jessie galloped off toward the bluff and sanctuary. Their horses, rested from the hard pace put on them before the ambush, took off with a sudden burst of speed and brought the bluff closer by the minute. A torrent of rain poured down, making the trail spongy and muddy. From off to the north, they heard a horrific, continuous booming sound as if the storm had changed course. Thundering and crashing toward them, a wall of water twelve feet high ripped up everything in its path as it bore down on the pair.

Sensing the danger, the palomino and sorrel picked up even more speed and made for high ground. The deafening roar hurtled toward them as they flew through the pelting rain. Jessie's heart pounded so hard, she felt as if she would never be able to breathe again. She held her breath and tried to make herself as light as possible to help the horse move even faster.

Suddenly she heard a sharp *clop* and then another. The horses had reached rock slabs and clattered their way up the foot of the bluff. Both horses jumped wildly from footing to footing, catapulting themselves and their riders away from the raging river bearing down on them. The higher they went, the quieter the impending torrent became. But the lightning bolts crackled around them, sparks flying and ozone heavy in the air, making breathing very difficult and gasping almost necessary.

With one last burst of effort, the horses found the high ground they had been straining to reach and trotted into a large crevice, a tall slice of stone wall that served as protection from the water and the storm. Jessie and Ki turned to watch the flood swoop by carrying uprooted trees and bushes in its wake. They shuddered at their close call, and Jessie patted her mare's sopping white mane affectionately as she dismounted.

Once they had a brisk campfire going inside the cave, they stretched out and prepared a little hot meal. As the storm blasted the world outside, they sat near the warmth of the flames and nibbled on their victuals. While they ate, the storm passed completely off to the east, revealing a breathtaking sunset that died quickly, bringing on a chill and a blanket of darkness studded with stars.

"In all the rush, I can't remember what made me think our bushwackers might not be Indians," Ki said. He sat in silence, rubbing his head as he chewed on the last of the hot meal.

"Has it come to you yet?" Jessie asked as they finished their food.

Ki rubbed his forehead. "It's right up here, waiting to be set free." He removed his headband and scratched his scalp around the indentation. "If I don't strain, it may come to me without my bidding."

Jessie smiled and leaned back. "Thank goodness for Tom giving us the long horses. That's the second time those animals have saved us."

"Horses! That's it!" Ki cried out. "Now I know what was bothering me. When I circled around behind what I thought were Indians, I saw something that just didn't fit. But there was too much going on for me to stop and figure it out at the moment."

Jessie nodded. "Yes, I know—the storm and the possibility of a flash flood, and then the ambush. It was a little unnerving."

"What I saw was horseshoe tracks in the earth near the bushwackers. Their horses had horseshoes, which should have told me immediately that these weren't Kiowa or any other kind of Indian. But my attention was focused on stopping their attack."

Jessie crossed her arms under her bosom. "Well, obviously, someone doesn't want us to get through to Wetumka. Or maybe someone just wants us dead." She shifted position. "Too bad about the flood. We could have learned a lot from the dead bodies." She looked out into the night. "I imagine their bodies are far to the south by now. You know, I could swear that the Indian who got away looked familiar, but I thought at the time that I must be confused by the storm and the ambush."

Ki looked deep into the fire's orange and blue flame. "And one of them got away. We'd better watch our step from now on, and stay off the main trail."

"You're right. It isn't safe anymore." Jessie spread out her tarpaulin and blanket and curled up in it, using her saddle as a pillow. "Let's get a good night's sleep and get an early start tomorrow."

Ki got up and took a look around outside before returning to the fire. Under normal circumstances, he would have stayed a moment to appreciate the clearness of the sky after a cleansing summer storm; the stars seemed almost reachable. Instead, after he made sure they were as safe as possible, he prepared his bed and rolled himself in the blanket and tarpaulin. "Good night," he said, his thoughts drifting off before he finished speaking.

Jessie and Ki slept so soundly that neither of them heard the crack of a dry branch broken underfoot just outside the cave.

★
Chapter 13

Stretched out in their blankets and tarpaulins on the cool, dry, sloping floor of the vertical opening in the bluff rocks of the Indian Nations Territory, Jessica Starbuck and Ki slumbered more deeply than they had in a long time. Not since they left Texas had Jessie spent a night of total relaxation and complete sleep. Before they bedded down, they had made sure the stone flooring beneath them slanted toward the opening so that water would not accumulate during the night. And as they lay in the blankets, two intruders made their way into the cave to take shelter.

One of the dead bushwackers' horses, having followed on the heels of Jessie and Ki's mounts, moved inside the stone crevice, drawn by a pool of water at the entrance and then by the warmth of the cave's fire. As small black bats winged their way out the top of the cave entrance, the stray black gelding nudged up to Jessie's palomino mare and whinnied softly.

Ki stirred, but only momentarily, and he fell back into a deep sleep. Jessie, exhausted from the night before, would probably have slept through an earthquake. As breathing grew steadier for Ki and Jessie, and the horses all but snored, no one heard the light clitter-clatter of tiny claws on stone. Sharp little claws, like fangs on a beast, ticked their way across the cave floor in search of a dark, warm shelter—a safe harbor after a tasty feast of frogs.

Jessica Starbuck's blanket caught the tarantula's fancy, and the gigantic furry black spider tapped its way under the warm fabric to settle in the crook of the slumbering honey-blonde's arm. Jessie, in the depths of a dream, felt nothing and slept on, never moving a muscle as the night slowly faded into day.

As the hours passed, the horses pawed the stone floor, their horseshoes clanging under Ki's head. He stirred and opened his eyes. The first bright light of day bounced off one of the vertical stone slabs at the cave's entrance and reflected in Ki's blurred morning vision. He rubbed his eyes and yawned.

When he sat up and looked around, he noticed the third horse standing near the others. If the flood had washed away the dead bushwackers' bodies, he thought, at least one of their horses might offer a clue to the gunmen's identities. He pulled himself out of his blanket and stoked the almost dead fire. Glowing embers caught on and created a small flame. He prepared the coffee pot for brewing, then approached the stray horse quietly, speaking gently to it, encouraging it to stay put until he could examine it for signs of ownership.

Jessie's sleeping body began to take notice of what was going on around her. Fire. Coffee. Ki talking to a horse? Little by little, her consciousness returned and she became aware of a new day—but just barely. Dazed but refreshed, and feeling much too warm under the light wool blanket and tarpaulin, she threw them off her and opted for another few winks.

Ki glanced down at Jessie but kept his attention focused on combing clues from the bushwacker's black gelding. But something in his peripheral vision disturbed him. Slowly, he looked around to see what was wrong—and saw, cradled in Jessie's arm, the largest tarantula he had ever seen, with a two-inch body and at least a five-inch leg spread. The hair on Ki's neck bristled as his mind raced to figure out how to dislodge the giant hairy spider without getting Jessie bitten in the process.

Before Ki could formulate a plan, Jessie's eyes opened and she yawned, about to stretch as she usually did in the morning after sleeping on an ungiving surface.

"Don't . . . move!" Ki whispered.

The urgency in his voice sent a chill through Jessie body, and her instinct to stretch reversed. She froze, her mind running through the possibilities of potential danger. Rattler? Scorpion? Centipede? Gila monster? Mountain lion? Indian? All could be deadly, but which was it? She controlled her breathing, inhaling slowly through her nostrils and exhaling even more slowly. She tried to keep from looking around or blinking.

"Tarantula!" Ki whispered. "On your arm . . . at the elbow."

Jessie's senses searched her arms and finally felt a weight in the crook of her right arm. By the feel of it, this seemed to be a very large one. Through her shirt sleeve, she could detect the slight prick of eight sharp-pointed claws. Her scalp involuntarily tightened, and a shudder ran through her body. Beads of perspiration welled up on her forehead and upper lip as she held herself rigid.

In the same urgent yet soothing whisper, Ki said, "Stay as you are—I'll take care of it."

Ki ran a gentle hand along the belly of the stray black gelding as he walked behind the horse. He couldn't chance spooking this unknown steed, but he had to find a long stick. Finally behind the three animals, he found a long branch that must have washed in the crevice during another even more vicious flash flood.

His razor-sharp hunting knife severed the smaller branches from the larger stock until he held a very long, thick pole. He whittled the tip down to a spike, working as quickly as he could. At any time, the slumbering tarantula might wake up and reject the cold morning air. And angered, it just might bite Jessie—right in the vein. He knew a tarantula's bite rarely proved fatal, but even the most general bite could make a man very ill. A small woman bitten in the vein might be laid low for a long time.

"Get ready to jump to your left." Ki approached Jessie's stiffened body from above her head. "I'm going to flick it off with this branch."

Jessie wanted to say something, to let him know she understood, but she didn't dare to even utter a sound. The rumble of an *uh huh* might disturb the spider. She waited, her eyes straight ahead, and tried to blink as infrequently as possible.

Ki slid the pointed branch down Jessie's shoulder to her arm, pausing just before touching the tarantula. Slowly, carefully, he pushed the pole to within a half-inch of the sleeping spider. He sucked in a deep breath and braced himself for the delicate maneuver.

"Now!" Ki yelled as he hooked the tip of the pole underneath the tarantula and sent the furry spider flying through the air.

Jessie rolled and jumped off to the left as the spider went sailing to the right. The honey-blonde stood crouched with her back to the cavern wall, rubbing her arms as if flicking insects off both limbs. Her left hand continued to flick off the tarantula that was long since gone. Reflex actions had taken over and she rubbed and rubbed. Very little frightened Jessie, and she could stand her ground against the worst of God's creatures, but waking up to a tarantula in her arms could ruin the best of days. A long shudder ran down her back.

The stunned tarantula landed on all eight feet, its long black-and-brown hair bristling. It scrambled to face Ki and Jessie, and circled to charge the humans, its claws clicking on the stone floor of the cavern. But the stray black gelding, spooked by the huge spider, reared and came down, its hoof squashing the arachnid so that only the thick furry legs showed.

"Coffee?" Ki asked, smiling.

Jessie shook her head. "Hug!" she said as she walked into his long arms. She stood with her arms around his waist, shivering for almost half a minute. Backing off, she looked up. "Now coffee."

While they sipped their coffee, they exchanged ideas and possibilities about the ambush. Strolling outside to view the damage wrought by the flood, they walked the three horses out into the sunlight. Not even the bright light of day helped Ki and Jessie to find a clue to the horse's owner. There was no saddle, and the makeshift bridle, used by many Indians, was merely a thick piece of braided rope that could have been made by anyone.

Ki said, "If we had time, we could follow this fellow home and find its owner." He motioned for Jessie to calm the animal. "Instead, I'm going to mark his hooves with my knife so that when we get back, we can trace his tracks."

Jessie held the rope around the horse's head while Ki lifted each hoof and carved a little X into it where it could only be seen from behind.

"Let's get going," Jessie said, tying down her bedroll to her palomino's saddle. "We have to make up for a lot of lost time."

Ki smiled. "Well at least the storm's behind us." He smacked the stray black gelding on the rump and sent the startled animal off onto the empty plains, hopefully to its owner. When Ki and Jessie got back to Harcourtville, they would easily be able to tell who owned the horse—or who had owned the horse.

Jessie watched the black horse race off into the distance. "I hope we don't have any more trouble on the way to Wetumka. It seems a little strange that a confidence man would have a gang of gunfighters—swindlers usually work alone or in pairs—and how would he know we were after him? On the other hand, I can't figure out who else would want to stop us from finding him."

"I know. It's puzzling."

★

Chapter 14

Graham Greenleaf and Archie MacTaggert swaggered into the First and Last Chance Saloon. They had already dropped a bundle at the Red Balloon Saloon's gaming tables and wanted to change their luck. They pushed open the swinging doors, and the acrid stench of strong red-eye, cigar smoke and sour sweat attacked their nostrils. Blue smoke hung heavy in the room, making it difficult to see from one end to the other. A rickety off-key piano rattled discordantly, but could barely be heard above the boom of voices—some laughing, others yelling, all at full volume.

Graham Greenleaf adjusted his fancy new coat and vest and caught a glimpse of his lean handsomeness in the ornate barroom mirror. He tilted his beige Stetson rakishly to one side and brushed his fine reddish mustache with the backs of his fingers. He smiled. Archie, half a head shorter than his friend even in his fancy new bowler, squinted at his own reflection just long enough to straighten his ribbon tie. As the dapper-looking pair sidled up to the bar to look over the tables of gamblers, the bartender stopped wiping the bar and shook his head.

"No more credit for you two," the ferret-faced man said out of the corner of his mouth. He raised his arm to motion for the bouncers.

Archie looked up at the bartender and said, "Hell, we don't need no credit, Sparky." He plunked down a fifty-dollar gold piece. "That should cover what we owe and drinks for the night."

Greenleaf, feeling expansive, flipped Sparky another eight-sided gold piece. "This is for you, my good man. Now please serve us your best rotgut and keep it coming. We have a full night of revelry ahead."

His jaw hanging slack, the bartender bit into the coin and then reached for a bottle from under the bar. His awed facial expression as he poured drinks for Archie and Greenleaf made both men snicker. They savored the aged liquor and smacked their lips. Whiskey tasted so much smoother when the price was right.

The tall confidence man pointed across the room. "Arch, let's sit in on Mitch's game—looks like he's got some real farm-hick pigeons there. We might as well get in on the plucking."

"You bet—roast pigeon, comin' up!"

Archie grabbed the bottle of prime booze and followed his friend to the other side of the room. He waited until Greenleaf sat before he eased himself into a chair next to him. Archie set the bottle between him and his friend and pushed his derby way back.

"I'm in," he announced, stacking a handful of double-eagle twenty-dollar pieces and several piles of single-eagle ten-dollar pieces in front of him.

"So'my," Greenleaf said, equaling Archie's stacks of single and double eagles. With great pride, the confidence man also slid a small heap of fifty-dollar gold pieces next to the others.

Mitch Montana, a snaggle-toothed professional gambler in his late thirties, scratched his filthy long brown beard and cackled. "Ooops! Looks like Greenie's oil wells came a gusher!" He laughed and slapped the table hard, bouncing cards and coins. He stared into the confidence man's cunning hazel eyes. "Think you can keep that luck going, do you, Greenie?"

"We'll see, won't we?" Greenleaf poured himself another glass of whiskey and sipped at it luxuriously as he held up one of the eight-sided coins between thumb and index finger. "Truth be told, these here are solid gold fifty-dollar pieces,

Mitch, old boy. Of course, we'll use the double and single eagles if fifties are too much for you—or we also got greenbacks, just in case you can't afford to keep up with us." He nudged Archie and grinned. "We wouldn't want to break him too soon, now would we, Arch?"

"Nope. Wanna make the fun last." The little man chuckled deep in his throat and looked around the table at the other players. "What's the ante?"

Mitch and the other players each tossed a five-dollar half eagle into the center of the table, and Archie and Greenleaf rummaged through their pockets to find a coin small enough. Archie flicked a half eagle into the pile, and Greenleaf exchanged a double eagle for three half eagles from the pot and placed them off to the side.

While Mitch opened a brand new deck of cards and shuffled well, Graham Greenleaf snapped his fingers and whistled for a waitress. Squirrel-tooth Sally rushed to his side and bent over him, hanging her pendulous breasts almost in his face. The bodice of her bright purple-and-red gown barely covered her, and her hennaed hair clashed with her dress and heavy lip rouge.

"What can I get you, Greenie, luv," she simpered, not really trying to keep her eyes off his stack of gold coins as she dangled her assets at him.

"How about the best cigars for my buddy 'n' me—long nines." He tweaked her breast where he thought her nipple might be and reached around to pinch her lace-covered bottom. He dug into his pocket and pulled out two quarter eagles for her, then took a fifty from the heap. "This here's for you. Make it quick, then stick around for good luck."

"Sure, Greenie," she said, bubbling, "whatever you say." She grabbed the coins and headed for the bar.

Mitch announced, "Seven card stud—nothing wild."

The professional gambler dealt the cards one at a time with a practiced hand, the first two in front of each player landing facedown. While the other six players waited until the two hole cards had been dealt, both farmers, wearing floppy-brimmed woolen hats, grabbed for their cards as they came and looked at them with anticipation and mild disappointment. The next four cards would be dealt faceup.

"All right," Mitch intoned, "Hank's got a deuce—too bad, Hank. Farmer Brown's got a ten. The devil's bedpost for Farmer Jones."

"My name is Jenkins, Joshua Jenkins, not Farmer Jones, and this here is my friend and neighbor Abraham Hobson." He looked puzzled. "And what's this devil's bedpost you talkin' 'bout?"

Mitch threw back his head and guffawed loud enough for the entire room to hear. "That's what we call the four of clubs, Farmer Jenkins." He continued to deal, sailing the cards faceup around the large table. "Your *four*'s not good for much, Farmer Jenkins. Whoa, Archie's got the ace of diamonds—look out for him. A trey to Greenie—that should be a real winner." He snickered. "Red's looking at the knave of clubs. Tommy's nine don't do nothing. And I get the knave of hearts—too bad, Red." He glanced over at Archie. "Ace bets."

Sally returned with cigars for Greenleaf and Archie and stood behind her benefactor, her bosoms resting on his shoulder. The confidence man lighted his cigar and puffed deeply as he watched his friend bet.

The little man in the bowler, holding an ace of hearts and the jack of diamonds in the hole, grinned and tossed two eagles into the pot. As Greenleaf thumped two coins down without even looking at his hole cards, Archie ripped the end off his cigar and spit it off to the side. He followed the betting as he sucked in a lungful of blue smoke and hoped something would come of his pair of aces.

Red McClintock unbuttoned the collar of his red-and-black plaid shirt, looked over at Mitch's jack and, finding no reason to stay in, prudently folded.

Tommy Tompkins chomped on his tobacco chaw and aimed a dollop of juice at the cuspidor next to him. He tossed in a double eagle, and Mitch peeked at his hole cards—an ace and a six of spades—then placed two eagles in the pot and waited for Hank Grayson, who also folded.

All eyes fell on the two poorly dressed farmers. Farmer Hobson held his hole cards—the king and ten of diamonds—

98

in his hand and studied all the cards on the table before finally dropping his coins into the pot. Farmer Jenkins, who held the queen of clubs and three of hearts, did the same.

Mitch dealt the next round of cards, calling them out as they fell. "Farmer Brown gets a seven of diamonds."

"Abraham Hobson, please," said the farmer, mustering his dignity.

"Yeah, right, Hobson. Farmer Jones—uh, Jenkins—gets the deuce of clubs. Uh oh, watch out everybody—he's got the beginnin's of a straight flush." He flipped over the next card for Archie and whooped. "Look out, fellas, Archie's got the puppy foot. That's a pair of aces showing, and who knows what he's got hidden in the hole."

Archie strained to keep a straight face but couldn't resist a loud yelp. "Here we go!" With his hole cards, he held three aces and was sure he could snag a pair of something to go with them.

Mitch continued the deal. "Six of clubs to Greenie— tough luck, Farmer Jenkins, Greenie's got your straight flush blocked."

At this point, Greenleaf put down his cigar and, making sure Sally couldn't see, took his first and only peek at his hole cards—the six of diamonds and the three of hearts. *Two pair already!* His pulse quickened by a few beats, but his facade remained as relaxed as ever.

Mitch continued, "Third two to Tommy, and I get a king to go with my knave—possible royal flush shaping up here. Pair of aces bets—watch him bump the pot."

Archie counted out four eagles and dumped them into the pot. "I bet forty dollars." He looked at everyone eagerly, obviously trying hard not to scare the others into folding. The potential for a gigantic pot loomed at him. Greenleaf dropped his four coins in, and Tommy folded in disgust. Mitch stacked four coins in the pot and looked impatiently at the farmer next to him.

Farmer Hobson thought about it, mulled it over, stared at the two hole cards in his hand, and finally plunked down four eagles on the strength of his pair of tens. Farmer Jenkins quickly slipped his coins into the center of the table and waited for the next card. After all, three clubs didn't make a flush.

Mitch dealt the next up card. "Pair of sevens showing to Farmer Br—uh, Farmer Hobson. Oh, oh! Five of clubs to Farmer Jenkins—that's lookin' more and more like a straight flush. Three of diamonds to Arch—sorry, old buddy. Five of diamonds to Greenie—possible straight goin' up against Farmer Jenkins's possible straight flush. And look out, boys, ol' Mitch's got a red lady to go with his king and knave— possible royal flush starin' at you. Pair of aces still in the driver's seat, Arch."

Archie squirmed in his chair and chewed messily on his long nine as he counted out six single eagles. "All right, let's separate the men from the boys. Sixty smackeroos." He shoved the coins dramatically into the center of the table and rubbed his hands together.

Greenleaf cocked his head, puffed on the stub of his cigar, and dropped six coins onto the center of the pile. "I'm in."

Mitch smiled. "And I boost you thirty," he said, counting out nine eagles and placing them carefully into the pot as he stared Archie down.

Farmer Hobson, his eyes wide, counted out nine coins. "I'm in." His voice wavered.

"Me, too," said Farmer Jenkins.

Archie and Greenleaf each added three more coins to the pot.

Mitch pushed back his sleeve cuffs and held up the deck. "Last card up—Farmer Hobson's got the spadilla, but that queen don't do nothin' for him, and it takes away from his friend's club flush. And so does this king of spades. Well, Arch, here's the curse of Scotland for you."

Archie looked down at the nine of diamonds and his eyes brightened. With an ace of hearts and the jack of diamonds as his hole cards, he had three aces or a possible flush, and maybe even a full house, if he got lucky. He wished Squirrel-tooth Sally would stand at his elbow for luck instead of behind Greenie.

Mitch continued, "Greenie gets a four and a possible straight—three, four, five, six—you got a bobtail showing." He flipped out his own last up card. "Jeez! Ten of hearts to go with the others. Possible royal flush growing more real by

100

the minute." He laughed. "All right, Arch, you're still in the driver's seat."

Archie counted out ten double eagles, and then ten more. "Possible full house bets twenty doubles—four hundred smackers." He looked around the table, challenging everyone with a leer, the stub of his cigar bobbing up and down between his clenched teeth.

Greenleaf blew several smoke rings and smirked. "I'll raise you two hundred. That's six hundred to you, Mitch, old boy."

"Here's my thirty doubles, and I bump another thirty," he said out of the side of his mouth. "Now it's twelve hundred bucks, folks."

Farmer Hobson gulped. "That's sixty double eagles to me? Oh, my!" He stared at his hole cards, at everyone else's cards, and finally counted out six stacks of ten coins. Two pairs just might take the pot, he figured naively. But it hardly mattered— just the thrill of sitting in on a hand with the famous Mitch Montana made it worth the price. This was an adventure he could tell his grandchildren about, and even if he didn't win, he would have lost to one of the greatest gamblers and gunslingers around.

Farmer Jenkins tried to keep from smiling, but the corners of his mouth twitched. "Sixty doubles to me, and I raise you a thousand dollars."

Everyone stared at the farmer, whose forehead now glistened with beads of sweat. Archie peeked at his hole cards again and sent up a massive smoke signal before reaching for five more stacks to keep him in.

"I'm in," Greenleaf said casually, shoving his stacks into the center of the huge pot.

"Me, too." Mitch shook his head and added another fifty coins.

Almost begrudgingly, Farmer Hobson counted out fifty more double eagles.

"Now it's down and dirty." Mitch Montana flipped the third hole card facedown in front of each of the four men still in the game and dealt himself one. "Archie? How'd I do yuh?" He chuckled throatily and spit toward the cuspidor. "You gonna bet or fold?"

Archie's grin tightened as he saw that the best he could do was three aces. "Two thousand dollars—that's one hundred doubles," he said, bluffing. Not much of a bluff, with his cigar suddenly cold in the ashtray. He pushed the coins into the pot.

Greenleaf counted out the stacks and added three more coins. "That's twenty-six hundred to you, Mitch."

"And I raise you another thousand." He pushed several stacks to the edge of the gigantic pile of coins and looked at the farmers. "That's three thousand, six hunnert to you fellas."

Farmer Hobson shook his head. "Thirty-six hundred dollars? Too rich for my blood. I fold—a couple of rounds too late."

Farmer Jenkins grinned from ear to ear, enjoying the moment. "Well, I call your thirty-six hundred and raise you a thousand more."

Archie was no longer smiling. "Hell, I might as well stay in to the end." He counted out several more stacks and then stopped. "To hell with it! I raise another four hundred." He pushed all the stacks to the pot.

Greenleaf hesitated. He knew Archie bluffed more than he didn't, so he discounted his friend's gesture. But Mitch just might have a royal flush, which would beat his full house by a long shot. And Farmer Jenkins might actually have a straight flush. But, feeling lucky with his latest oil well stock sales, he counted out stacks of coins. "And I raise you a thousand more."

Mitch knew his ace-high straight beat Greenie's probable eight-high straight, so he quickly raised another thousand and waited.

Farmer Jenkins couldn't remember if a straight beat a flush and was afraid to ask. On the off chance that his club flush might take the pot, he called.

Archie blanched and called. Greenleaf raised another two hundred just to be ornery, but everyone called him. He rubbed his hands together and puffed feverishly on the tail end of the cigar. Then he proudly turned up the three hole cards that combined with his first two up cards to make a full house. No one could match his hidden full house, and no one had guessed that's what he had held.

"Dammit, Greenie!" Mitch bellowed. "I'll get you! This time it's gonna be straight draw poker!"

Greenie giggled as he raked in the coins—hundreds of coins, close to forty thousand dollars, he reckoned—and stacked them in front of himself. He handed Sally a couple of stacks and kissed her hand as she scooped them up. "You're an angel on my shoulder, beautiful." He flipped her another eight-sided coin. "Drinks for the table—the best."

Faces lighted up at the mention of good booze.

Still stacking coins, the confidence man said, "Truth be told, it was a pleasure doing business with you, Mitch, fellas! Now let's get down to some serious poker."

★

Chapter 15

Jessica and Ki crossed the Cimarron River at a point where it seemed the easiest to ford and followed the meandering waters southeast for many miles, keeping a wary eye out for bushwackers—white or Indian. They felt fortunate to be able to keep water within sight, but knew they would soon be forced to leave the river's protective shores and travel due east to Enid. At that time, they would have to forage for water holes in the dry plains of sagebrush and tumbleweed. Until then, they could provide their horses with all the water they required.

As the pair rode along, they spotted groups of windowless Indian log huts with mud roofs lining the riverbank. White smoke wafted from a central hole in each hut's rounded mud-thatched roof; squaws sat in front of their huts, grinding corn and tending to food preparation. Infants tied to their mothers' backs watched intently as if learning a valuable lesson from others around them, while toddlers practiced standing and walking, and frisky dogs sniffed around for scraps.

Friendly Cherokee, after having been forcibly removed from Georgia fifty years before when the white man discovered gold on Cherokee land, had settled in this territory of what was called the Five Civilized Nations. From what Jessie and Ki had been told, the Cherokee settlement extended for some distance, and just below it was the settlement of Waynoka, one of the last refuges of civilization for the white people—a stagecoach line with all the amenities of the East: telegraph and mail service.

The closer Jessie and Ki got to the straggling settlement, the more they could see of its inhabitants. Dressed in whatever scraps of used clothing they could scavenge from the white people, they wore combinations of outfits that appeared to the white eye as ludicrous. To the red eye, it was purely utilitarian. Warmth and cover, nothing more—except for bright colors, which were aesthetic.

Jessie and Ki rode into the middle of the community, greeting the people they passed. They had been told that below the Cherokee community, just before they reached Waynoka, they must leave the river and travel eastward. They swung off their horses to replenish their canteens for the long trip to Enid, the first stop on their trek to Wetumka and the oil country.

"I'll water the horses and fill the canteens," Ki said, "and then we can have a snack before heading east." He glanced up into the sky. "It's almost lunchtime, and I could stand a little something."

"Sounds good to me," Jessie said, watching the women and their babies.

While the horses drank their fill and Ki dipped the canteens into the sparkling river, Jessie wandered over to a group of Cherokee women and bade them hello in sign language. They greeted her tentatively, curious about a paleface female dressed in men's clothing. Her large light green eyes and curly golden hair contrasted greatly with the squaws' coarse, straight blue black hair and small black eyes. Fascinated by Jessie's long flowing honey-blond tresses, the Indian women asked in sign if they could handle it.

"Of course," Jessie signed, smiling and removing her hat for better access.

The women held her hair and stroked it gently. One of the squaws gingerly brushed Jessie's long dark-blond lashes from side to side, fascinated by the curl and resilience of such lengthy eyelashes. Then another of the women offered to let Jessie hold her papoose.

"Thank you," Jessie said, taking the plump infant in her arms.

The baby grinned at Jessie and burbled, and the women all laughed. Another mother, who wore a battered old Stetson, brought her infant for Jessie to hold, and Jessie put the first one on the ground to crawl around. Soon Cherokee papooses filled the grassy area, pulling at one another and exploring on hands and knees or experimenting on inexperienced legs, while mongrel dogs romped between them and allowed their ears and tails to be pulled.

As Ki approached, the women openly stared at him. His exotic looks confused them—he was not one of them, but he was obviously not a paleface either. He wore his long black hair straight instead of plaited, kept in place by a braided headband—just like the Cherokee braves. But while his hair was black, it looked as soft as the female's and held a tinge of brown, not blue. His high cheekbones and almond-shaped eyes lent his face a Cherokee look, but his light skin's coloration bore a trace of pale yellow.

While the people crowded around Ki, braves almost as interested in him as were their women, Jessie watched from a distance, still bouncing a child in her arms. Ki knew a few words of Cherokee, and with that and sign language, he held a lively conversation with the people clustered around him. The women faded back as their men spoke with Ki, and Jessie lowered the papoose to the ground. One of the pet mongrels ran up to lick the baby's face.

The dog cleaned off all uncovered areas of the child's skin and headed for the next toddler. Suddenly, the dog stopped in its tracks, staring straight ahead into the rocks where a toddler was practicing to walk. The dog growled from deep within its throat, its ears back, and its lips curling up into a vicious snarl.

Jessica froze. One of the papooses had crawled off and was trying to pull himself up by holding onto a boulder. As his wobbly legs stiffened under him, he locked his knees and rocked back and forth before falling. When he fell, he disturbed a snoozing snake. Rattles high, the alarmed snake coiled, preparing to strike.

Oblivious to the imminent danger, the toddler swayed, trying to stand again, fascinated by the sound of the rattles. He leaned toward the snake, grabbing for the snake's tail. The dog barked, yapping and crying, but the rattler, unaware of the helplessness of the extremely young human reaching out for it, inched its head back for what would surely be a fatal strike.

"Ki!" Jessie yelled as she quickly drew her .45 Colt revolver and shot twice with deadly accuracy, severing the rattlesnake's head from its body. Her cry had been a reflex action, a means of gaining Ki's attention just in case she might miss and need backup. "Never mind," she said as she raced over and swept the sobbing papoose into her arms to comfort him.

The Cherokee people crowded around Jessie, all talking at once. The dogs jumped up on her, licking her hands and arms, apparently trying to show appreciation. The toddler's mother took her baby and cradled him in her arms, trying to calm him down. The noise of the shots and the barking had frightened him, and someone had broken his "toy." One of the braves picked up the rattler's body and head and held the pieces up for all to see.

"Golden Eagle," Chief Running Buffalo proclaimed Jessie's Cherokee name in sign language. She would forever be known as Golden Eagle, the yellow-headed one who struck down the grandfather of rattlesnakes and saved the community's precious Raging River. "We are always in your debt," he signed, "for your eagle eye, accurate gun and big heart."

Although Jessie and Ki wanted to leave and be on their way, the people of the Cherokee settlement would not hear of it. Before the two could leave, they must accept a meal of celebration and friendship or risk insulting the entire community.

"We have to eat, anyway," Jessie reasoned.

Ki said, "Yes, and it would be an affront if we left before letting them share their food with us." He nodded to the chief and walked with him to the eating area. To Jessie, he said, "We can make up time later."

The sun reached midheaven and then dipped slowly into the west as Jessie and Ki finally made their way to their horses and mounted up. It was probably two in the afternoon, they estimated, and they had a long ride before nightfall. After many warm farewells, Jessie and Ki came to the last of the Cherokee huts at the southern end of the settlement and then struck off due east toward Enid. Far in the distance to the south, they could see the homes of Waynoka.

The trail east, lightly traveled, showed little evidence of water supply. Unlike the path along the river, this one had few trees and fewer bushes. Sagebrush and tall dried grasses grew between clumps of dusty dirt. Fortunately, the sun bore down on them from behind, rather than baking their faces. The ground on either side of the road looked almost white, which meant they were close to the salt flats. They rode hard, trying to make up for lost time again.

After a long stretch of constant gallop, they slowed their horses' pace to rest them. As they went along, they chatted to fill the time.

"You know," Jessie said, "I've heard two different versions of how Enid got its name."

"Oh? I've only heard one."

Jessie mopped her forehead with the dusty handkerchief and pulled the wide brim of her hat even lower on her brow to shade her eyes from glare. "Someone told me the town was named after the founder's wife, whose first name was Enid."

Ki shook his head. "That's not what I heard."

"Well, the other version was that the mayor named it after an epic poem by Tennyson—'Idylls of the King,' so they said."

Again, Ki shook his head, his long black hair swaying on his shoulders. "Nope."

Jessie looked over at him, tilted her head, and raised an eyebrow. "All right. You're just dying to tell me. Go ahead—what's your story?"

Ki smirked. "I got this from a completely unimpeachable source," he said, toying with her. "You really want to know, do you?"

"Oh, forget it," she said, laughing, feigning disinterest.

"All right, you don't have to beg. I'll tell you." He cleared his throat dramatically. "It seems that a while back, some of the drovers riding into the unnamed settlement after a long cattle drive, had a few too many drinks and shot up the place. There was only one sign in the settlement then, and it hung over the cook's tent and read Dine. Well, someone shot at it and knocked it upside-down. No one ever bothered to fix the sign, so everyone started calling the place Enid—Dine backward." He chuckled. "And that's the truth." He shrugged his shoulders. "It's as good as naming it after someone's wife or a poem."

Jessie laughed and kicked her palomino's sides, ripping off into a gallop. "Let's race!" she called as her mare took off like the wind.

"Good idea," Ki yelled into her dust.

The two took turns chasing each other, heading toward Graham Greenleaf's hometown. They sped past another cluster of Indians and gave silent thanks that these also appeared to be members of one of the peaceful tribes. No one tried to stop them, and few paid much attention to a voluptuous young woman with long honey-blond curls and a tall, lean Asian with equally long black hair.

The trail suddenly branched off to the south, but Jessie and Ki had expected the fork and kept going straight ahead on the eastern branch. Neither path had been much traveled of late, but they both noted that at least four shod horses had been on the eastern path quite recently. The tracks appeared extremely fresh.

Ki held up his hand, motioning Jessie to slow down. She tugged gently on the reins, causing her palomino to break its gallop into a halting canter. "It may be nothing," he said, "but those hoofprints are too fresh. We should have seen their dust, but I can't see riders or dust up ahead."

"Yes," Jessie said, pointing to some trampled sagebrush, "that's less than an hour old." She stood in the stirrups and raised herself up on the saddle for a better view of the trail ahead. "No, no dust and no riders anywhere." She pulled her horse to a walk.

Ki shook his head as he slowed his gelding to a walk. "I may be getting skittish after so many bushwackings, but I think we may be heading into another ambush right now." He looked around for cover, and she surveyed the area for good places to ambush someone.

Jessie said, "Up there." She pointed to an outcropping a few hundred yards ahead on the left. "That's where I'd hide to attack someone traveling east."

110

Ki nodded. "You're right. That's where I'd ambush someone if I had a mind to." He looked the trail over and said, "Just to be on the safe side, let's circle around that outcropping. If there's no one there ready to attack us, we've lost a few minutes. If bushwackers are waiting, we'll bypass them or outrun them."

Jessie and Ki turned their horses around and backtracked a few yards and then abandoned the path off to the left. Circling around far behind the outcropping of rocks, they quietly made their way to a point several hundred yards beyond the ideal ambush spot. They hoped nothing would spook their horses and call attention to them before they got out of rifle range.

Patiently keeping their horses reined in, they cut back and found the trail to Enid and continued along it, picking up speed as they put distance between them and the outcropping. The path appeared unused, no evidence of fresh hoofprints whatsoever. Once they felt sure they had averted the danger, they allowed their mounts full rein and sped along at a mighty gallop.

The farther east they went, the more trees they saw. It seemed as if they were leaving a desert and approaching lush woodsy land. The trees became more plentiful and larger—there had to be water somewhere nearby. As they rode, they watched for signs of a water hole or a creek.

Ki pointed. "Up ahead," he called out. "Looks like a water hole." He surmised this from the number of trees in a cluster and the tall green grass and abundant bushes surrounding the trees. "Time to rest the horses," he said, heading his sorrel toward the stand of trees.

Jessie nodded and followed Ki toward the trees and a possible watering hole. "Go on, I'm with you," she yelled into his dust.

Suddenly, several shots broke the stillness, and Jessie's pale palomino staggered, a rifle bullet penetrating its neck, another its rib cage. As the mare stumbled and fell, Jessie grabbed her rifle and leaped to safety. She crouched in the tall grass and waited for the shooting to stop. Ki turned his sorrel and rushed back to pick up his lovely companion, but more shots from the other side of the trees whizzed by his ear. He slid from his horse and dashed for cover in the tall grass.

111

★

Chapter 16

"You hit?" Ki rasped, not able to see Jessica through the tall grass.

"No, but Beatrice is down," Jessie whispered just loud enough for Ki to hear. "If she isn't dead, we'll have to put her out of her misery once we extricate ourselves from this." She turned her attention to the rifle shots that zinged by overhead.

Again, the pair split up, one ducking far to the right, the other off to the left in a pincer movement. They hoped to catch the bushwackers in a deadly crossfire.

"Fan out!" a deep voice yelled from beneath the trees at the source of the rifle fire. "They're on foot."

Jessie got the range on the first verbal order to fan out and fired her Winchester when the gunman called out the second time. A *splat* echoed in the vicinity, followed by a gurgle. Then silence.

"Harvey?" a gravelly voice asked. "Hey, are you all right?"

Jessie focused on the direction of the initial call, and shot as he asked his question. Another *splat*, this time followed by a strangled cry of pain. More silence, except for the sound of a meadowlark off to the right. Jessie recognized the familiar birdcall—Ki was letting her know he was now in position.

Rifle shots sounded from near the trees, rapid and loud, but well off-target. Jessie inched closer, waiting for Ki to attack.

113

She could hear one of the men muttering to himself, but he wasn't speaking loudly enough for her to home in on his voice and pick him off.

"Goddamn them!" the gunman muttered. "They got Harvey *and* Blackie. Well, they ain't gonna get me. I'll show 'em! That bitch ain't gonna get away from us this time—and that Chink is gonna meet his maker. Come on, bitch."

Jessie and Ki both heard the muttering and could barely make out what the gunman was saying. But they both noted that the speaker had mentioned a "bitch" getting away before. These were no ordinary road bandits—these were bushwackers out specifically after them. Perhaps even part of the same group that had masqueraded as Kiowa warriors during the storm and tried to massacre them on their first day out of Harcourtville.

Jessie waited for Ki to act, but when she didn't hear anything, she decided to step up the hostilities. She picked up a large rock, big enough to get someone's attention but small enough to raise overhead and throw. She held the rock high in the air and tossed it side-armed into the bushes at the base of the trees.

"Goddamn it! You sonuvabitch!" the mutterer yelled. "I'll get you for th—"

Again, Jessie focused on the first expletive and fired on the second. She caught him midword and midheart. A rustling in the grass to the left of the fallen gunman meant there was at least one other gunman still alive. Ki would take care of him, Jessie mused.

Ki, realizing what Jessie was doing—sighting on first words, shooting on second—crept up behind the fourth bushwacker and let out a sharp cry as he kicked the man in the back of the neck, jerking the head one way and the body another, snapping the spine like a twig in a storm. The bushwacker died before his limp body hit the ground.

"All right," Ki called out. "Unless they have someone hidden well out of range, that's all of them. Just four this time."

Jessie stood up and looked around, straining her ears to hear anything foreign. Nothing but critters resuming their life on the plains.

Ki examined the four bodies, checking through their pockets for information about the bushwackers. Once he pulled their neckerchiefs off their faces, he could see that all four wore beards, and one of the gunslingers looked familiar. In fact, that one looked a great deal like one of the two nasty bruisers who had confronted them on their first day in Harcourtville.

Jessie smoothed out Beatrice's dusty white mane and removed the decorative sterling-silver bridle and bit from her foaming mouth. The wounded horse panted and watched Jessie's every move, snorting from pain. Gently, Jessie pulled at the cinches and released the saddle, wresting it from the mare's back. Pink froth bubbled forth, and the sight of Beatrice suffering tugged at Jessie's heart.

Under the stand of trees, Ki pulled a note written on expensive white stationery from one of the gunmen's pockets and unfolded it. Suddenly he heard another shot. He sprang into action, dashing toward the sound.

"Ki, it's all right," Jessie called out in a tight voice. "That was me—sorry, I should have warned you first, but I had to end Beatrice's misery."

"Maybe one of the bushwackers' horses is still here. If not, we'll have to double up." Ki headed off to where he thought the horses might be tied. "You get the saddle off while I round you up a new mount."

"I already have," she replied softly.

Ki wandered around within a few hundred-yard radius and finally found horses tied to a small tree. "I found 'em. There's five to choose from—" Five? There's still one bushwacker out there somewhere! Ki thought. He swung himself up on a large bay gelding, planning to rescue Jessie, but dismounted quickly and circled around through the tall grass as quietly as possible, tying his sorrel and the gunman's bay to a tree out of sight of the other horses.

Her hands full of saddle, and her mind preoccupied with sorrow, Jessie didn't hear the bushwacker approach until it was too late.

"Drop the saddle, bitch," the gunman rasped into her ear as he clapped his left hand over her nose and mouth from behind, "or you're dead where you stand."

Jessie's body went rigid. She could not cry out for help. A little muffled cry didn't carry very far, she knew—not far enough to warn Ki.

"No, I ain't gonna shoot you yet," the bushwacker whispered. "In fact, I got a knife here in your back. Make some noise, and I shove it in—right between the ribs." He jabbed her in the kidney region just hard enough to make his point.

The stench of putrid breath sent a chill through her. It smelled familiar—she had smelled it before. But there again, many roughnecks in the West did little more than smoke or chew tobacco, drink cheap whiskey, and vomit. Jessie squealed and tried to wriggle free.

"Goddamn you, bitch! Drop the saddle now!"

She knew why he hadn't killed her yet. He was using her as bait to lure Ki. He planned to kill them both, but he didn't want to go up against Ki alone. With her as a shield, he had a chance of shooting Ki before killing her. She had to think of something.

"Drop it!" he rasped.

The bushwacker poked her hard with the sharp tip of the knife for emphasis, and she jumped. As she let go of the saddle, tossing the heavy mass of leather as far away from her feet as she could, she kicked her captor in the shin with the heel of her boot. His grip on her mouth tightened as he swore under his breath. Instead of stabbing her as he had promised, he brought the knife to her throat and laughed a low, mean guffaw.

"You try that again, bitch, and you're dead meat on the spot. My boot's too thick for your girlie business." He kept the knife at her neck as he glanced around for her oriental companion.

Jessie let her body go limp, giving her captor the impression that she had given up. She knew she could outfox him if she got him offguard.

"That's better." His nose nuzzled her hair. "You smell awful good, you know. Too bad I can't have a little fun with you before I finish you off. You're not a bad looker, you know."

Taking his lead, Jessie wriggled her hips and ran her hands along his thighs. Her firm buttocks ground into his groin, and she could feel his body responding. She moaned lightly, clinging to his body, her nostrils smarting from the proximity of

116

his foully sweating body. But her hands got too close to his holster, and he brought his knee up into her buttocks hard.

"Stop that, damn it!" he snarled softly.

His fingers bit into her cheek and cut off all air from mouth and nose. She grabbed his fingers and pulled, trying to get a breath.

"I'm gonna let go now, and I want you to call the Chink to come on over here." He squeezed her hard. "No funny business, or else. You warn him and you're dead."

Her captor released her mouth, pressing the point of the knife into her smooth neck, pricking the flesh slightly and drawing a drop of blood.

She gulped a breath of air and nearly gagged from the sickening odor of her captor. She forced herself to open her mouth to yell, but the bushwacker pricked her again.

"Call him!"

Before she could say anything, she heard Ki's meadowlark call telling her he was aware of her position and was somewhere nearby. He would take care of this bushwacker. She stood still and waited. Moments later, she heard the *zing* of a throwing star, and she fell back onto her captor. She knew that if she moved forward, the bushwacker's knife would sever her jugular vein. Instead, she lurched in the cutting direction and twisted toward him so that she faced him nose to nose.

Ki's *shuriken* sliced into the arm holding the knife, and the sudden pain caused the bushwacker to pull his arm away from Jessie. As she spun around, Ki delivered two karate chops from behind to the base of the bushwacker's neck at the shoulders. His knees buckled, and Jessie jumped out of the way just in time.

"What took you so long?" she asked, smiling.

Ki shrugged. "I got here as soon as I realized there were five horses and only four dead bushwackers." He looked her over for signs of harm. "Sorry I didn't take him out sooner, but I had to make sure he was waiting for me before I acted."

Ki yanked the knife from the ambusher's hand while Jessie pulled the six-shooter from the man's holster. Ki knelt with his knee in the middle of the gunman's chest and waited for him to regain consciousness. A few hard slaps on the cheeks helped.

Jessie looked down at her former captor. "Why, that's one of the roughnecks from Harcourtville. See?" She pointed at the side of his head. "No ear."

Ki nodded. "Yes, didn't the marshal call him Spike? I also recognized the other one, the one they called Buck. He's over by the trees."

"Why are they trying to kill us?" Jessie asked rhetorically.

"We're about to find out right now. He's coming around. Good morning, Spike, did you have a nice nap?" Ki slapped the man's cheeks once more for good measure.

"Go to hell!" the bushwacker spat. "Both of yuh!"

"You'll be there before us—but not until you tell us why you're after us and who's behind it," Ki demanded.

"You sonuvabitch, I'll be goddamned if I'll tell you anything!"

"Tough guy," Jessie said, "even when he's about to die. You have to admire that in a man, Ki. Here he is, ready to meet his maker, and he puts up a mean front." She smiled, taunting him. "Of course, Ki can kill you quickly with one blow to the right spot, or he can draw out the pain and let you die a slow agonizing death I wouldn't wish on an Apache renegade." She bent over, holding the knife to his neck. "I wonder which he'll choose, Ki. Fast or slow?"

"Yeah," Ki said, "he reminds me of that stupid outlaw we caught in Thunderhead, Colorado. He acted so brave and talked so tough, and died whimpering—all because he chose the slow death instead of telling us where the money was." He laughed cruelly. "And just before he died, he told us anyway. What do you want to bet, Jessie, that the people in Thunderhead still remember his screams?"

Jessie chuckled. "Oh, yes, and I bet they'll never forget you. But why make it slow? Let's just kill him and get it over with. Who cares why or who's out after us? We're wasting time here. Let's just put him out of our misery and get on our way to Enid."

Ki looked up at her and frowned. "Don't tell me what to do! If I want to kill him slow, I will. What's your damn hurry?"

118

"He held a knife to my throat!" she yelled. "That's what my hurry is!" She drew her six-shooter and aimed it at the bushwacker's head.

"Stop that!" Ki hollered. "I want to know what he knows. If you kill him now, we'll never get anything out of him. Now you go over there and stay out of my way."

Jessie's eyes glared at Ki as she cocked the revolver.

"Who do you think you are, ordering me around!"

Ki jumped up and reached for the gun, but it went off and he grabbed his upper abdomen, staggered, and fell forward onto his face.

"Oh, my God!" Jessie cried. "Ki!" She dropped her six-shooter at her feet and cradled Ki in her arms, rocking him and cooing to him.

The bushwacker called Spike saw an opportunity to get away. His knife and gun were under Ki's body, but if he could get away before the blonde came out of her shock and shot him, he might have a chance. He considered hitting or kicking her unconscious, but she still had her gun and might use it. He thought better of attacking her; he would simply slip away to fight another day.

As Jessie held Ki's motionless head in her lap and rocked him, Spike crawled off into the tall grass and worked his way around to the horses. He found four tied to the tree, so he mounted his and slapped the other three. Even when the blonde did realize he was gone, without a horse, there was little she could do about it. And she would probably die before she got herself to civilization.

Spike laughed out loud as he rode off toward Harcourtville to report on his victory. The Chink was dead, and the girl was as good as dead. He'd get a bonus for sure, and maybe even a promotion.

As soon as Jessie heard the hoofbeats pass and fade off into the distance on the westward trail, she dumped Ki's head off her lap. "Get up. He bought it."

Ki pulled himself up. "I hoped you'd remember how we hoodwinked that outlaw in Thunderhead by staging my death. When the audience is on the ground, looking up, it really appears that I've been shot—unless the bullet were to hit

119

something directly behind me. Of course, your acting ability helped, too."

Jessie laughed. "While we're praising each other, you make a marvelous dead body."

Ki went for the two horses he had tied to a tree far from where the bushwacker would have looked. He had planned to use the ploy right from the moment he realized one of the gunmen was still alive.

They transferred Beatrice's saddle to a bay gelding and continued their journey to Enid. Now they knew for a certainty that someone was out to stop them. And Spike's report would be most misleading.

Ki said, "We may have outsmarted that one-eared fellow, but those other bushwackers were pretty smart, purposely leaving the trail where they did, diverting our suspicions so we'd run right into their ambush." He shook his head. "And it almost worked."

"Yes, but now we're aware of their intentions, whoever they are." Jessie adjusted herself in the saddle. "If, for some reason, their boss doesn't buy our little skit, then we just won't go anywhere near places where an ambush might occur. If we stay off the trail, go straight through the brush and keep away from any paths, they won't be able to anticipate us."

Ki pulled a piece of white stationery from his jeans pocket. "I forgot all about this—a note I found on the body of one of the bushwackers." He read in silence, then read it out loud: "It says, 'Jessica Starbuck, blond, green eyes, medium height, well built, good shot with rifle and six-shooter.'"

Jessie nodded. "That's me, all right, but they forgot my good teeth."

Ki smiled and continued, "'Ki, oriental, long black hair, black almond-shaped eyes, thin mustache, very tall, martial-arts master—beware of his bare hands and feet.'" He chortled. "Very interesting."

"Someone knows us and wants us dead. There isn't any letterhead, but that would be too simple." Her laugh was hollow. "Is the note signed?"

"Yes," Ki answered. "Down at the bottom, I can just make out a name." He looked at it closely, shifting it around to get

120

better light on it. "It says, 'B . . . O . . . S . . . '" He shook his head. "I can't make out the last letter. Here, see if you can."

Jessie took the note and held it up to the sunlight and studied the signature. "You're right. That last letter is hard to . . . Oh, for Pete's sake! The last letter is an S. It says Boss. Now that tells us a whole lot, doesn't it!" she said in bitter sarcasm.

★

Chapter 17

Graham Greenleaf looked at his dwindling stacks of coins and gulped. After that first gigantic pot he'd won, he could barely find room for all the coins he'd raked in. Now his stacks of coins were nearly where they had been when he started. Although he was not broke, he was not the big winner he had hoped to be.

He reached for the bottle of fine whiskey, but it was empty. When he called for another bottle, Squirrel-tooth Sally refused to go for it without another large coin. He had already tipped her more than several cases worth and reflected sadly on how cold she could be when his piles of gold coins shrank. He tossed her another eagle and consciously kept from making a face.

Mitch Montana, whose luck had changed, was winning and said, "It's Hank's deal. Is everybody in?" He looked around the table. "If not, ante up."

He waited for the players to ante, looking pointedly at the two farmers, waiting for them to give up their seats at the table so some other pigeons with fresh bankrolls could take their chairs and enjoy the thrill of losing to a professional gambler and possibly watching a shooting should someone get caught cheating. But the two farmers whispered between themselves and apparently agreed to stick out just one more hand before leaving.

"Hank's deal," Mitch repeated, handing the deck to the bald man to his left. "Dealer's choice. What's yer pleasure, old buddy?"

Hank Grayson took off his crumpled black Stetson and wiped inside the headband with a much-used kerchief. Frowning, he said, "No more of this here funny business—for the last three hands, I had to sit and wait for all you ladies to finish piling up your money. I came here for two reasons—to win some cash, and to have me some action." He picked between the few teeth he had left with a hand-whittled toothpick. "This time it's gonna be draw, nothin' wild, jacks or better."

With shaky hands, the gaunt oldtimer shuffled the cards one last time and shoved them to Mitch to be cut. As Hank dealt each player five cards one at a time, the farmers grabbed for their cards almost before they hit the table. When Hank finished dealing, both farmers had their cards in hand and sorted, their faces mirroring their reactions to their hands—one good, one bad.

No one at the table missed this sign of the amateur, but only Mitch seemed to be disturbed by it. He chomped down on his chewing tobacco and spit loudly, missing the spittoon. He coughed and hacked as spittle went down the wrong pipe, choking him.

"Goddamn sonuvabitch," Mitch grumbled. More than anything, he wanted to tell the two nestors to skedaddle, but he calmed himself and refrained from an outburst that might cost him a big pot. He took in more from amateurs like the farmers than from playing with the usual regulars. He might treat them with a small amount of contempt, but he refrained from showing how he really felt.

Hank looked at Farmer Hobson. "Can you open?"

The farmer stared at his cards and then at Hank. "Well, I—"

"You got a pair of jacks or better in your hand or don't yuh?" Hank growled.

"Oh, a *pair* of jacks or better," the farmer repeated, finally understanding the terminology. "Why, no . . . I have no jacks at all."

Losing patience, Mitch said, "It don't have to be jacks! Do

you have any pairs or any combination that'd take . . . uh, beat a pair of jacks?"

"No." He put the cards down in front of him.

Hank said, "Then jes' say pass."

Farmer Hobson picked up his cards again one at a time and said, "Pass!"

All eyes fell on Farmer Jenkins.

He gulped. "I—I can open." He took a coin from his remaining stack. "One eagle—that's ten dollars."

"We know," said Mitch, Hank and Tommy in chorus through clenched teeth. Hank's toothpick broke from the pressure, and Mitch spat and missed the spittoon again. He wiped his mouth on the back of his sleeve.

"Well," Farmer Jenkins said, "I bet ten dollars." He placed the coin in the center of the table and withdrew his hand quickly, as if afraid it might get chopped off by one of the professionals.

Archie tossed a double eagle in the pot. "I raise you ten."

Greenleaf, watching with mild interest, kissed the palm of Squirrel-tooth Sally's hand for luck as she placed the new bottle of sippin' whiskey next to him and removed the empty bottle. He tossed a gold eagle into the pot without saying a word and filled his whiskey glass. The smooth liquor burned a little on the way down, and he sent Sally for a meat sandwich.

Everyone else followed suit, with the farmer adding another eagle. Then Hank picked up the deck and called for cards.

"How many?" he asked Farmer Hobson.

"One card, please." He put his discard in front of him and pounced on the card Hank dealt him, but his face dropped when he looked at it. "I fold," he said, discarding the hand faceup on the table.

Mitch hollered, "Don't you never fold with your cards up, damn it!"

The farmer blanched and flipped all his cards facedown, his hands shaking. "I'm sorry. I didn't know."

Hank looked at Farmer Jenkins. "How many?"

"None for me, thank you." He tried to keep a straight face, but his lips quivered and he bit down hard on the insides of his

125

cheeks to keep from smiling or laughing out loud with excitement.

Farmer Hobson, surprised at the pat hand, tried to see his friend's cards, but Farmer Jenkins kept them too close to his chest for the first time that evening.

Archie tossed three cards toward Hank. "Gimme three beauts." The three new cards to go with his pair of fives did not improve the hand. He considered bluffing, but thought better of it, since even Farmer Jenkins's opening hand could beat his pale pair. "I'm out," he said, throwing down his hand in the discard pile.

"I'll take two," Greenleaf said, placing his discards in front of him. He drew to a straight and missed by a mile. "Fold." He tossed his hand with the discards.

"Gimme two," Red McClintock said. The two red cards ruined his possible club flush, and, his cheeks florid, he folded in disgust.

Mitch folded when the two cards he drew to his original three face cards made nothing.

Hank Grayson also folded when he couldn't make his bobtail into a full flush. He turned to Farmer Jenkins. "You win—the pot's yours, since everybody's folded. But you gotta show us your openers."

Joshua Jenkins displayed his hand on the table in front of him one card at a time. He held an ace-high straight—all spades, except for one club.

Farmer Hobson slapped his friend on the back. "That was good playing, Joshua! You won a pot!"

Farmer Jenkins glowered at Abraham Hobson as he raked in the few coins from the pot. "Yes, I did, didn't I? In the last two hands, I lost over eight thousand dollars. And now I win a spectacular two hundred dollars—twenty-five of which I put in the pot to begin with. Some winner!"

Archie piped up, "Yeah, but now you can say you won a pot offen Mitch Montana. Not too many folks can say that."

Greenleaf, sipping his whiskey faster, said, "Come on, are we gonna chew the fat all night or what? It's your deal, Farmer Brown."

"You mean, I get to deal the cards?" the farmer asked incredulously.

Archie laughed. "Yeah, and you get to choose the game." He nudged Greenleaf. "You gonna choose Old Maid or Go Fish or Spit in the Ocean?"

"I'm going to sit in two more hands, I think. And we're going to play the same as this last time."

Greenleaf thought to himself that the game would be a lot more exciting once the farmers left and they could get back to stud poker with new suckers. That's where the big pots were, and with his luck going the way it was, he should break the table before the night was over.

Archie leaned over and whispered to his friend, "Oh oh, don't look now, but there's Hollie Hollingsworth over by the bar."

Greenleaf lighted another long nine, then glanced over at the bar and saw the notorious gunslinger watching Mitch and Hank. The confidence man hoped he and Archie could win a few more hands, make their fortune, and get out before the trouble started. Hollie Hollingsworth, he reflected, was hell on hooves and probably the meanest sonuvabitch west of the Mississippi. If he sat down before they left, they'd have to stay indefinitely. And Hollingsworth could be hazardous to one's health.

Both Greenleaf and Archie straightened their stacks of coins, preparing for a quick getaway when the lead started flying. There were enough other clubs and gaming tables in town, and they didn't need to be where Hollingsworth might start something.

"You goin' somewhere?" Mitch demanded.

The two startled men jumped perceptibly in their chairs and grabbed for their whiskey glasses, shaking their heads and gulping down the fiery fluid to calm their nerves. It wouldn't be healthy to cross Mitch either, so they settled in for a long night.

Greenleaf puffed languorously on his cigar, smiled his oiliest flimflam smile, and looked Mitch right in the eye. "What would give you that idea, Mr. Montana? Truth be told, I was

127

just straightening up my coins—getting ready for another big pot."

"Yeah, me too," Archie said without conviction, fidgeting with the coins.

"Greenie," Mitch boomed, "you 'n' yer little buddy ain't leavin' this table till I get a chance to get back some of my money. Ain't no way Mitch Montana is gonna get hit and run! Got that?"

Archie said, "Yessir!"

Greenleaf nodded, and somehow the fun had gone out of the game. Even Sally's breasts on his shoulder felt more like dead weight than the sensual delight they had earlier in the evening. To make sure Mitch didn't accuse him of cheating, the confidence man took off his coat and rolled up his sleeves—just in case.

All of a sudden, an evening's distraction had become a game of life and death. Greenleaf reached for the whiskey bottle, hoping to blank out the rest of the night.

★
Chapter 18

Jessie and Ki checked in at the only hotel in Enid, attracting
a great deal of interest. Several cowmen ambled into the hotel
lobby to get a better look at the big green eyes and huge rounded breasts. Not very many women rode through Enid, and those
who lived there were either painted whores or penitent wives.
Jessie's presence caused quite a stir among the townfolk.

At the hotel front desk, Jessie signed the register and asked,
"Do you know Graham Greenleaf? I was supposed to meet him
here this morning, but I'm a little late."

The wizened little desk clerk looked at her blankly, then
called the stiffly dressed hotel manager to the front desk. "Mr.
Laughlin, these two people were supposed to meet Greenie
here this morning. Have you seen him?"

Mr. Laughlin looked Jessie and Ki over very cautiously, his
face evidencing no sign of recognition.

"Greenie, Mr. Laughlin—you know, Graham Greenleaf?"
the desk clerk said, trying to be helpful.

"Uh, yes, Derrick, I know who you mean. It's just that
I . . ."

Jessie understood the manager's reticence. "As we explained
to Mr. Derrick, we were supposed to have met Greenie here
this morning—but we had trouble on the road and just arrived.
I hope we haven't missed him altogether—it would have been
mutually profitable." She looked up at the hotel manager with

her most forlorn facade, from under drooping lashes.

"Well," the manager said, softening, "I would be the last one to keep Greenie from making a dollar." He hesitated, opened his mouth, then thought better of it.

Jessica's face brightened, and her smile all but knocked Mr. Laughlin over with its glow.

"He stopped here only for a moment a day and a half ago and then headed straight for Wichita. From the looks of his bulging luggage, though, he made a big haul this last time out." He grinned at Jessie. "You'll find him at the Red Balloon or the Last Chance—those are his favorites. But if you don't get there soon, he'll be flat busted—no matter how much money he took in."

Jessie fluttered her lashes. "Thank you so very much, Mr. Laughlin. You've been such a help."

As soon as the manager left to busy himself in his office, the old man called Derrick said, "If you have trouble finding Greenie, just locate Archie MacTaggert—they're old buddies and almost inseparable. Archie owns a print shop in Wichita. Can't remember the name of it now, but just ask anywhere—everyone knows Archie."

Jessie and Ki had their sparse luggage in hand and turned to go up the staircase when the desk clerk read the registration card.

"Jessica Starbuck?" he asked. "That's you, right? Well, I'll be dogged! Miss Starbuck—there's a couple of telegrams that's been waiting on you. One's from Oklahoma City, and t'other's from someplace called Harcourtville . . . I guess it's out west." He grinned as he held out the two folded pieces of paper to Jessie.

"Thank you very much, Derrick. How efficient of you," she said breathily as she took hold of the telegrams and glanced briefly at the one from Oklahoma City. She and Ki would read them both thoroughly in the privacy of her room, where they could discuss them freely.

The old man's cheeks flamed, and he found himself at a loss for words and completely under Jessie's spell. He started to say something, but words wouldn't come. He stood looking at her.

130

"By the way," she added, "when's the next train to Wichita leave here?"

Derrick blinked, obviously saddened to hear she might leave town so soon. He scratched his shaggy head as he thought about it. "Let's see, today's Wednesday, right? That means the next one's day after tomorrow—Friday, at about noon."

Ki cut in. "How about the stagecoach?"

"To Wichita?" the desk clerk asked.

"Yes, to Wichita."

"Leaves tomorrow mornin' at about seven." He smiled, proud of his wealth of information. "And it's a Concord—real comfy."

Jessie and Ki thanked the desk clerk, ascended the stairs, and went to her room. She unfolded the first telegram—it was another from Halleybelle and Bert Harcourt. And this one was also urgent.

DEAR JESSICA:
    LAWYER MAXWELL BLEDSOE BEHIND EVERYTHING. STOP. URGENT YOU RETURN QUICKLY. STOP. WATCH OUT FOR AMBUSH. STOP. BE VERY CAREFUL. STOP.
                                    H & B HARCOURT

The second telegram, from the territorial capital in Oklahoma City, indicated that Maxwell Bledsoe and the Harcourtville Bank had been buying up land for miles around Harcourt County. What Bledsoe and the bank hadn't bought outright, they held mortgages on—and were foreclosing the moment the mortgage payment was late. For some reason, few of the mortgage holders were able to meet their payments, and with the exception of some very large ranches and farmland, Bledsoe owned it all.

Jessie shook her head. "I knew it. That Maxwell Bledsoe was much too cooperative, so softspoken and genteel. But I wondered at the time why the bank founder's grandson was not president of the bank . . . and his oldest friend and attorney was. It just didn't smell right." She stretched and yawned. "Let's get an early night's sleep and catch the stagecoach for Wichita in the morning. I think it would be a good idea for us

131

to bring that confidence man back just as soon as possible—especially before he squanders all his loot."

"Well," Ki added, "let's just hope that 'Greenie' hasn't already lost all the cash. Some of those card games have pretty high stakes, from what I've heard. If he hasn't lost all the money, I think I have a plan to get everyone's money back."

"Good, because I'd been considering something that just might fix the wagon of whoever it was who's been doing all this to the people of Harcourtville and us. Now that we know the culprit, maybe between the two of us we can come up with a powerful payback for lawyer Bledsoe and his gang of seedy cutthroats."

Ki headed for his room. "See you in the morning. Get some good sleep tonight."

Early the next morning, Jessie and Ki caught the Concord stagecoach to Wichita. Thurmond, the driver, assured them that since there were only two other passengers on the coach besides themselves, and one of them was getting off halfway, at the Kansas border, he and his assistant could bring the stagecoach on in without stopping overnight just above the border. If he and his assistant took turns and drove straight on through, they could get to Wichita late the next day—if Jessie, Ki and the remaining passenger didn't mind sleeping in the carriage overnight.

Jessie offered a hefty bonus if the driver and his assistant could get them to their destination before the sun set the following evening. With dollar signs dancing in his head, the sturdy young driver pulled his scrawny assistant aside for a short talk, then slapped the horses and took off at full speed, planning to get his money's worth out of the horses before trading them off at the way station on the Kansas border.

Jessie and Ki eyed the passengers sharing the stagecoach with them. One was obviously a farmer returning to his home after a visit to Oklahoma City. When he saw Jessie enter the carriage with the help of Ki, he removed his woolen hat and sat twisting it in his lap. Before she could be seated, he jumped up and gave her his seat facing forward.

"Please, take my seat, miss," said the farmer in an obvious Germanic accent. "I've seen enough already, and I'm almost to mine home. You might as well face forward. I'm sure the gentleman next to me will also give his seat to your companion."

The farmer stared into the other passenger's eyes as if ordering him to vacate his seat to Ki. Without emotion, the other passenger got up and plumped himself down next to the farmer, facing backward. After thanking the farmer and the other man for their graciousness, Jessie settled in and studied the silent man. He wore a black suit, black Stetson and black leather boots. He didn't appear to be wearing a holster, at least not a hip holster. But he did carry a black leather briefcase of sorts. It ran through both Jessie and Ki's minds that this man might very well be another of Maxwell Bledsoe's killers sent to stop them.

Jessie and Ki exchanged wary glances, each silently telling the other to be careful. The pleasant, roly-poly farmer posed no threat, but the gaunt man in black might.

Jovially, the farmer said, "Please, let me to introduce myself. I am Heinz Stoltzer, and this is . . . " He looked at the man next to him and waited.

"Enoch Cadwalader," the man in black said sullenly.

"I'm Jessie and this is my associate Ki."

All four fell into a pensive silence, and Cadwalader was the first to break it once the carriage got under way. "Are you going to Wichita, my daughter?" asked the slender man in his late forties.

Before Jessie responded, she noted that this man was not looking at her the way most men did—not the way the farmer stared at her longingly. She had on a delightfully low-cut lime green traveling dress with matching shawl, bonnet and handbag. Most men, she knew from experience, found it difficult to keep their eyes from straying to her deep décolletage. The farmer all but ogled her openly. The other man, however, never once glanced down at her inviting breasts or her nipped waist.

Ki also noticed this beady-eyed man's lack of interest in Jessie's pulchritude. The *te* master sat alert, ready to pounce should the man draw a weapon. There appeared to be a definite danger here.

Finally, Jessie answered Cadwalader's question. "Yes, my friend and I are on our way to find an associate of ours who's staying in Wichita." She smiled prettily. "You might know him—Greenie Greenleaf?" She looked at both men to see if there was a glimmer of recognition.

The farmer laughed. "Very colorful, this Greenie. But I don't know him. Of course, there is no reason why I should. I spend most of mine time on the fields. Behind a plow is not the place to meet people."

The pale man in the dark clothing shook his head, his facial muscles never relaxing. "No, I can't say that I have ever heard that name before. What does this Greenleaf person do in Wichita?"

"He's a salesman," Ki said, "a very good one from what we hear, but we've been told that he's up there gambling at the moment."

At the mention of the word *gambling*, Enoch Cadwalader flung open his briefcase dramatically. Ki quickly reached for a *shuriken* from his vest pocket but waited to see what the dark stranger would withdraw from the leather case before throwing it.

Through clenched teeth, the pale man in black menaced. "That is precisely why I am going there! Wichita is a vast den of iniquity—the devil's playground—that must be rendered unto Gawd!" From the briefcase he brought out a gold-embossed Holy Bible, which he shook at Ki. "Heathen—heed the word!" he yelled, thumping the book. "Gawd watches you and Gawd knows you to be a sinner! But Gawd loves you and He can save you. Accept the Lord Jesus Christ in his Savior's name. You will be twice blessed."

Startled by the outburst, the plump Heinz Stoltzer jumped and moved his bulk closer to the window. Apparently, from his facial expression, Cadwalader had treated him to a sermon most of the way from Oklahoma City.

Ki gripped the *shuriken* even tighter, flippantly wishing to end the tirade that he knew was forthcoming and would probably go on for hours. His sympathy went out to the unfortunate farmer, and he felt sure the poor tiller of the earth would be thrilled to take his leave of the stagecoach and the traveling preacher.

134

Finally, Ki let the throwing star drop back into his vest pocket. He smiled and waited for Cadwalader to take a breath so he could let him know that he was a Christian. Once Ki shared his unorthodox upbringing with the man—who turned out to be an evangelist from Oklahoma City—the two of them got along famously, sharing anecdotes and killing time, while the farmer scrunched as far into the corner as possible and tried very hard to doze.

Jessie rested her head against the leather cushion behind her and slipped off into a delicious half-sleep. The carriage lurched and swayed rythmically, and she fell into a much deeper sleep, one of dreams. In her dream, she and Bert Harcourt rolled over and over in the biggest bed she had ever seen. They were both delectably naked, and he kissed her all over, from head to toe, front and back, his tongue reaching areas she never dreamed he could or would as he tantalized her. She moaned in her sleep, and the men thought she must be having a nightmare. They could not have been farther from the truth.

In her dream, the honey-blonde spread her legs far apart as Bert teased her blond furry patch and licked at the dewy fluids there. Her body shuddered as his tongue nearly drove her mad with ecstasy, his lips sucking at her excited flesh, his teeth affectionately nipping at her more sensitive places. This was all hers—without him saying so, she knew he wanted her to relax and let him do it all. She obeyed, delighting in his dominance. There would be time later for her to take over and show him what ecstasy really was, but for the moment, she lay perfectly still as he traced her hot flesh with his tongue and lips.

He took her fingers and sucked softly on each, teasing the pad of each finger, stroking her palm with his tongue as she ground her pelvis toward him and pleaded for his presence. His moist lips slid down to her wrist, lighting on her pulse and quickening it, then on up to the inside of her elbow. His mouth on her fluffy patch had not excited as much as this—it was almost sheer madness.

Jessie moaned louder as the handsome man in her dreams sucked and licked and stimulated her responding flesh almost to the breaking point. She could feel her body coiling from the direct stimulation, readying itself for that unbelievable moment when the tension would snap and she would sail off into sexual glory. Her muscles tensing up, she whimpered as her body built toward a climax.

"Jessie! Are you all right?" Ki asked, alarmed by her apparent nightmare.

Both the farmer and the preacher stared at her, sincere worry on both their faces.

Ki shook her. "Jess, are you all right?"

Jessie opened her eyes and tried to bring herself into the present. It was difficult, very difficult. Her body was still in a dream state, but it felt as if someone had poured cold water on her before she could experience that powerful release she had been looking forward to, had been hurtling toward.

"No, I'm not all right!" she snapped and turned away from Ki.

Ki sat waiting for her to explain as the other two men looked on in silence.

"I'm sorry," she said softly. "I guess I was dreaming. Yes, I'm sure I was." She looked at Ki and the others apologetically. "I didn't mean to snap. Really, I'm just fine. A little unsettled from having suddenly been yanked out of a very delightful dream so abruptly—before it could be resolved."

"Then it's my turn to apologize," Ki said. "Please, try to return to that time and that place—go back to sleep. I'll be here when you wake up." He smiled knowingly. "Pleasant dreams."

"Thank you," she said as she closed her eyes and rushed back into Bert's arms.

★
Chapter 19

Maxwell Bledsoe sat behind the solid oak desk in his lavish law offices, stoking up his favorite cherrywood pipe. The large man's penetrating brown eyes looked out from under bushy, overhanging silver-and-black brows as he glared at Spike Randall. Curls of bluish smoke floated toward the ceiling, but the bruised and disheveled gunman looked only at the toes of his boots.

"What do you mean," Bledsoe demanded menacingly, "they've been taken care of? Four more of you knucklebrains get yourselves killed, but you survive and get the drop on the woman and the oriental. Then instead of finishing them both off, you frantically sneak away like a whey-faced yellowbelly when the blonde 'accidentally' shoots her bodyguard in an argument over *you*?" The lawyer's harsh laugh bounced off the certificate-laden walls and would have smacked the unhappy hired gun between the ears—if he had had two ears. "Do you really think the Chinaman is dead?"

"Well, sure, boss. I seen him get it right in the gut. *Bam! Ugh!* And the Chink goes down like a ton of bricks. *Thunk!* Then the dame starts with the waterworks. *Boo hoo hoo!*" He grinned broadly. "She really fell apart, Boss. How else do you think I coulda got away?"

Maxwell Bledsoe looked ceilingward. "Give me strength, oh Lord! Why do You surround me with complete idiots!"

He ground his teeth into the pipe stem, almost severing it, and puffed until Spike nearly choked from the aromatic smoke cloud fast enveloping him. "Listen, you poor imitation of a jackass, those two connivers *let* you get away! You blasted imbecile! They wanted you to think you'd escaped so you'd come running back here and report them dead, don't y'know." The attorney smacked the palm of his hand down on the desktop for emphasis. "By gum, with a lesser man than I, they might have succeeded. But Jessica Starbuck will never outthink Maxwell Bledsoe!"

"Not hardly!" Spike said in an attempt to ingratiate himself.

Lawyer Bledsoe glared. "They questioned you before they staged that death scene, didn't they? Well, what did you tell them? Did you tell them anything about me before you 'escaped'?"

"Hell, no! 'Course not! Whaddya take me for, anyhow?" Spike scowled. "They coulda cut off my other ear or stuck my feet in a fire or cut out my tongue—and I still wouldn'ta talked!" he said proudly.

"Oh, God save me from such ignorance!" The attorney fell silent and pulled at his silvery muttonchops, muttering to himself, "I wonder what they're up to."

Spike shook his head. "I don't know, Boss. I still think they're done for. It was just too real. They're both dead by now." His scraggly bearded face brightened. "Besides, even if they was still alive when I left, how could they get outta there without no horses? Remember? I told you, I slapped all the other horses so they'd run off. So even if they lived, they'd be stuck where they are till their bones bleach."

The attorney looked up at the hulking gunman, his eyes riveting the scar-faced man. "And can you remember just how many horses you scared off?"

"Yeah, sure." Spike held out his hands and counted on his stubby fingers. "I recollect there was three I chased off, cuz when I got back to the tree to get my mount, there was four there." He beamed with pride. "I 'member thinking at the time that one of the ponies musta broke loose, cuz there had been five tied to the tree when we first got there." He counted on his fingers again. "Yeah, that's right. There was five of us, and we each had a horse. But there was only four horses when I took off."

"Oh? So one of your horses ran away?" Maxwell Bledsoe spoke through clenched teeth. "And how many horses did *they* have?"

"You mean, the blonde and the Chink?"

"No, I mean Mother Goose and Little Boy Blue!" the lawyer exploded in frustration. "Of course, I mean Jessica and Ki, you dunderhead!"

Spike looked confused. "I forget the question."

"How . . . many . . . *horses* did the oriental and the woman have between them?"

Spike smiled, pleased with himself. "Two—but I shot the dame's horse out from under her, so they only had one left between 'em."

"More's the pity, I don't know why I even bother . . . but if you only saw four horses—three of which you scared off before you rode away on the fourth—what happened to the other three?"

The gunman counted on his fingers again.

"Spike, seven people arrived at that spot before the shooting started—all on horses! So there had to be seven horses to start with, don't y'know. You shot one of the horses out from under the blonde, and that makes six damn horses."

Spike's face fell.

"What happened to the other two goddamn horses, you lummox?"

The burly man shrugged his shoulders and looked at his employer blankly. "Maybe they ran away?"

"How convenient! Two people left behind to die—one with a bullet wound in his abdomen and the other without a horse. But if there just happened to be two horses stashed off to the side, which of course you wouldn't see, they could ride off to their destination just as soon as you're out of sight, now couldn't they?"

The attorney banged his pipe into the ashtray so hard a chip of the ceramic flew off and nicked the gunman in the arm. Spike did not flinch, not even as blood trickled down his knuckles and onto the oriental rug. Three times he had failed to get

139

the job done, and even with his limited intelligence, he knew his boss had little patience left.

"I'm sorry, B—"

"Shut up! By gum, I recognized those two as trouble even before I met them. That Starbuck woman is well known for her law-and-order antics. She's out here to help the Harcourts, and that's the last thing in the world I want!" He changed pipes, opting for a larger one—his prized carved meerschaum—and stuffed it full of tobacco shreds. "If that woman and her half-breed friend hadn't come up here, I'd own the whole goddamn county by now—and more! And it wouldn't be long before I was governor of my own state!" His voice trailed off to a whisper. "Or president of my own country . . . "

Spike's eyes grew wide.

"Now, with those two meddling into my affairs, I have to waste time trying to get rid of them." He took time to light his pipe, pulling hard on it until he inhaled a mouthful of aromatic smoke and let it curl into the air.

"I'll get 'em this time, Boss."

"More's the pity, Spike, but I bet you think you can." He shook his head, and his voice softened. "Go send the marshal over here. I want to speak with him. Now!"

The burly gunman lumbered from the room and, within minutes, brought back Marshal Teddison, with his deputies in tow.

"Ah, Roscoe, come on in," Maxwell Bledsoe said, smiling and motioning Spike out.

Marshal Roscoe Teddison pushed back his tall hat and sank into the chair facing the attorney. "You wanted to see me, Maxwell? I brought my deputies, Sandy and Clint, just in case we need 'em."

"Thanks, but they can stay outside with Spike. This is between the two of us, don't y'know." The lawyer leaned over the desk as far as he could and lowered his voice. "That Starbuck girl is still alive! Three separate attempts, and no success yet! I've lost eight men so far, and by now those two know something's up."

The marshal shook his head. "Too bad you didn't put me in charge. I'd have finished them off the first day by letting Buck and Spike take 'em on by surprise, and then I could have

140

called it a fair fight started by the Chinaman." He pulled a long, crooked stogie from his well-worn vest pocket and rolled it between thumb and fingers. He sniffed at it before wedging it between his back teeth. "It woulda been nice and clean and fast."

"And heavy-handed and obvious," Bledsoe said. "No, Roscoe, there are dozens of honest people in this town who would swear the pair had been bushwacked. That Starbuck girl has too many friends in high places." He leaned back in his chair and blew some lazy smoke rings. "No, now that the ambushes have failed, we must be subtle. I've told Quincy over at the telegraph office to let me read all messages going in or out of Harcourtville—especially those to and from the Harcourt place or the Starbuck gal."

The marshal nodded. "Good thinking. Have you found out anything yet?"

"I think so. Unless Spike is right—and, by gum, there's more chance of me sledding in hell—they're trying to find Graham Greenleaf, which they mustn't do. If they ever get a chance to speak with him, sooner or later they'll be able to figure out what happened here." He inhaled deeply and watched the smoke rise as he exhaled. "I just intercepted a telegram from the Harcourt kids to the Starbuck girl, pleading with her to come back because I'm involved in their problems, don't y'know. They mentioned me by name!"

"Oh, boy! That's not good!" the marshal said, chomping down on his stogie.

"On the contrary, Marshal, that falls in with my plans. If I know those two, they'll head right back here to rescue the Harcourts—before getting a chance to speak with Greenleaf. And they'll wire the Harcourts to let them know they're on their way, don't y'know." A dirty laugh rumbled up from deep within him, sending a chill through the grizzled town marshal.

"I presume that's where I come in?"

"By gum, you're bang on! Yes, this time I want some men who know what they're doing to finish that pair off. I've lost too many men as it is. I figure you and your deputies could stop one little woman and one scrawny oriental before they make any more trouble."

141

"No problem, Maxwell. They're as good as six feet under. No one will ever know what happened to 'em." He grinned and lighted his stogie. "Just give us the word, and we'll take care of 'em—with pleasure."

Maxwell Bledsoe stood, reached across the desk for the marshal's hand, and shook it with conviction. "By gum, I knew I could count on you."

As soon as Marshal Teddison got back to the jailhouse, he gathered all his deputies around and explained their assignment. He had a lot of planning to do, and he needed some input. After the three recent fiascos, he wanted to make sure that his deputies succeeded where Bledsoe's henchmen had failed. The more fully prepared his men were, the better their chances of getting the job done right. After all, what could be so difficult about killing one frail woman and a scraggly Chink? His deputies were all professionals, weren't they? The marshal felt certain he and his men would come through.

★
Chapter 20

When the stagecoach from Oklahoma City and Enid pulled up in front of the Hotel Sedgwick, three very sore passengers alighted. The traveling evangelist gave his blessing to the other two and wandered off, Bible in hand. While Ki collected the luggage, Jessie gave the driver two large coins, and one for his assistant, and thanked him profusely for getting them to Wichita just a little after noon.

If they located Graham Greenleaf in time, she reflected as she joined Ki on the way into the hotel, they could be on the next train south before the day ended. But a room was essential—to change, clean up and rest in. Even if they only stayed an hour or two, they would still need a hotel room—and a comfortable one, at that.

Men and women stopped to stare at Jessica Starbuck. Her tight-fitting lime-colored gown emphasized all the right curves, and the neckline showed off her ripe breasts. The women appreciated the outfit's coordinated color scheme and the fancy Paris finishes of the gown and bonnet, while the men rushed into sexual fantasies.

Oblivious of the stir she caused, the body-weary honey-blonde looked as fresh as if she had slept in a royal bed all night. "Let's drop off our luggage here at the hotel and change clothes," Jessie said, "and then start searching for Greenleaf."

"Good idea," Ki said, looking haggard from lack of sleep. "We can't get to bed until we find that swindler . . . and his loot."

Jessie nodded and headed into the hotel lobby. At the desk, they both registered, and she asked for a two-bedroom suite if they had one. Dazzled by Jessica's radiance, the desk clerk looked through all the slots and came up with the hotel's best suite.

"It's the presidential suite," the young gentleman said pretentiously, hoping to impress the lovely blond damsel before him.

"Oh?" Ki asked. "How many presidents have stopped over at this hotel?"

The clerk looked stumped, then rushed on, "I know you'll enjoy your stay with us. If there is anything you want . . . anything at all . . . please don't hesitate to ask." He stared into Jessie's big green eyes. "I'd be more than happy to take care of it myself."

Jessie and Ki grabbed their keys and headed for the staircase, forestalling the speech that usually followed. A bellhop dashed in front of them and took their bags from them as he plucked their keys from their hands.

"Follow me, please," he said efficiently and led them up the wide flight of thickly carpeted stairs to massive double doors at the end of the first corridor. "Right this way, please." He turned the key in the lock and pushed the doors open wide. "The presidential suite," he said dramatically. "If there's anything—"

"Yes, thank you, we'll let you know," Ki said, handing the young man a dollar.

"Thank *you*, sir!" He rushed around, opening windows and fluffing pillows before finally exiting backward, his eyes on Jessie's bust.

Ki smiled and then yawned. "Well, let's clean up, have breakfast, and find that Greenleaf fellow so we can get this case over with."

They sponged quickly in their separate rooms and changed clothes. Jessie put on her lavender-and-gray riding outfit, and Ki changed into a clean cream-colored shirt and dark cotton pants.

144

In the small restaurant attached to the hotel, Jessie and Ki ate a modest breakfast and quizzed the waiter about Graham Greenleaf and Archie MacTaggert. The waiter, flustered by a woman in men's jeans and cotton shirt—and holstered six-shooter—tried without success to explain how to get to Archie's print shop. In frustration, he called over the maître d' to help him out.

After the stiff maître d' collected his thoughts—he, too, found himself astonished by the lovely young woman in men's clothing—he gave Jessie and Ki detailed instructions to get to the shop.

"But," he added with his nose in the air, "from what I hear, Archie closed his shop two days ago. He's been in an all-night poker game at the First and Last Chance Saloon with Mitch Montana and Greenie Greenleaf—and *Hollie Hollingsworth*." He spoke as if Jessie and Ki should know who all three men were.

"Thank you," Jessie said. "By the way, who is Hollie Hollingsworth?"

The maître d' gave her a startled look as if she might be less than intelligent or from another planet. "Hollie Hollingsworth is probably the meanest, nastiest gambler in the West!" he sniffed. "He arrived in town last night, and he's been sitting in on the game ever since." The man's lips pursed into what some might consider a smile. "And he hasn't killed anyone yet."

"But he will?" Ki asked.

The waiter jumped in. "Oh, you can bet on that, mister. There ain't been a game that Hollie's sat in on yet that didn't have at least one poor cuss carried off with a good case of lead poisoning."

"Then why would anyone play with him?" Ki asked.

"Nobody really wants to," the waiter continued, "but once he sits down, he don't allow nobody to leave the table 'less he says they can."

Ki and Jessie stared at each other with a look of utmost urgency.

"Thank you, again," Jessie said, dismissing the two men. "Ki, we'd better get to that game. It's fortunate no one's been killed so far."

On their way out, they asked the desk clerk for directions to the saloon and were told it was just a block away. They made their way through the clusters of people staring at Jessie in her jeans and gunbelt, arriving at the saloon just in time to hear raised voices coming from within. Jessie had planned to remain outside until Ki flushed Greenie out, but from the sound of the conflict inside, Graham Greenleaf's life might be on the line. She followed on Ki's heels as they dashed through the massive swinging doors into the darkened room.

"You dirty sonuvabitch!" someone at one of the poker tables yelled. "I'll fix your wagon! You dealt from the bottom—I saw you do it!"

Sparky, the bartender, stood as far away from the table as the bar would let him. He said almost to himself, "Oh, oh! There goes Hollie."

Jessie leaned over the bar and asked, "Which one is Hollie Hollingsworth?"

Sparky looked at her for a moment. "Hey, lady, you're not supposed—" He shrugged. "Hollie's the one what's doin' the hollerin', that's who."

Jessie rasped, "Ki—stop him!"

Ki rushed into action. In two flying steps, he landed like a panther right behind the furious gambler. As Hollie reached for his twin six-shooters, Ki brought the sides of both hands down in a karate chop on his shoulders at the neckline. The large man crumpled into his chair, limp as a kerchief.

Tommy Tompkins reached for his weapon where he sat, but Ki flicked the man's chair out from under him with one swift kick. The chair's leg splintered, and Tommy tumbled to the floor.

Mitch Montana jumped to his feet, his chair flying backward, and went for his revolver.

But Jessie already had hers aimed at him. "Don't," she yelled, "please don't make me shoot you."

"Oh, yeah?" Mitch laughed. "Sparky, what's this dame doin' in here?" He drew his six-shooter and leveled it at Ki's stomach.

146

★

Chapter 21

Jessie didn't miss a beat. Her Colt .45 went off, knocking the gun from the gambler's hand and making a nasty mess of two of his fingers. "Now everyone sit down and relax," she said calmly as she approached the table, her six-shooter aimed at Mitch's chest. "I think it would be a good idea if you all were to put your weapons where my friend and I can see them, if you don't mind"—she smiled, but her eyes were cold—"and even if you do."

Ki walked around the table, motioning for each of the players to put everything on the table and clasp their hands behind their necks. Red McClintock dropped a large bowie knife and a Colt .45 on the felt in front of him, a deadly scowl on his face as he reached for the back of his neck. Ki gingerly lifted Hollie Hollingsworth's six-shooters from the unconscious gunfighter's holsters and stuck them in his own belt.

Mitch picked up his revolver with his left hand and gingerly dropped it on the table before retrieving his chair and uneasily raising his hands. Each man in turn put at least one weapon in front of him, until the table was filled with hardware. One dapper chap placed a pearl-handled derringer in front on him.

Jessie walked up to him. "Greenie? Graham Greenleaf?" she asked.

"Why, yes. Do I know you?" the handsome confidence man said eagerly.

147

"No, but I know you," she said breathily. "Would you mind coming with my friend and me? We need your help badly." She hoped her smile would dazzle the swindler enough to get him outside without a struggle. "Please?" she said, her voice overflowing with promise.

Graham Greenleaf's penetrating hazel eyes appraised the honey-blonde, and he came to a quick decision. "Excuse me while I collect what's mine." He turned to the table and scooped most of his stacks of coins into his jacket and trouser pockets and the rest into his hat. He returned his miniature weapon to a vest pocket and shrugged at Mitch. "Well, fellas, I guess I'll be going now. Sorry I couldn't stay longer—you know how much I hate to leave while I'm ahead by this much."

"Oh, sure," Mitch growled.

"Hey, I'd really love to hang around and give you all a chance to win back your money, but the lady needs me, and who can turn down a damsel in distress?" He chuckled lightly. "Besides, I really don't care to be here when Hollie comes to. 'Bye all." He glanced back and motioned with his head. "You coming, Archie?"

The short man in the bowler shoveled all his coins from the table into his derby and followed his friend without a word. Graham Greenleaf strutted past Squirrel-tooth Sally and Sparky the bartender and out through the swinging doors with Archie at his side. Ki kept close behind them, while Jessie slowly backed out, her six-shooter poised and ready to open fire.

Once outside, Greenleaf stopped and asked, "All right, now what in hell is this all about? You two kind people realize you just saved my life in there . . . so whatever you want—you've got it."

"Within reason," Archie added, feeling a little safer in the light of day with the weight of so many coins jingling in his hat.

Jessie nodded. "It's true, Mr. Greenleaf, we do need you. In fact, we need help from both of you. Let's go back to our hotel, where we can tell you all about it. I'm sure you'll find our proposition interesting and difficult to turn down."

Once in the Sedgwick suite, Jessie and Ki could explain their

148

problem and their need without fear of being overheard. Secrecy was of prime importance. If even one word of what they had planned was to get out, the entire scheme would fall apart, and Maxwell Bledsoe would win—and everyone in Harcourt County would lose.

The four sat facing one another, Ki and Jessie sitting on the plush chesterfield and Greenleaf and Archie lolling in large, comfortable overstuffed chairs. The two swindlers relaxed in the luxurious setting and waited to find out what this was all about.

After she and Ki had introduced themselves, Jessie asked, "Mr. Greenleaf, did you ever wonder why all the customers on your last trip west bought so much more stock from you than usual?"

Greenleaf nodded. "I most certainly did! Truth be told, I was puzzled every step of the way." He glanced at Archie. "At one point, I thought for sure that it was some kind of setup for the law to trap me." He shrugged his shoulders. "Well, what would you think if every pigeon you plucked asked for more—in some cases, begged?"

"You can thank Maxwell Bledsoe for that," Ki said.

"Who?" The dapper confidence man looked confused. "Am I supposed to know the name?"

Ki nodded. "He advised them to buy more. In fact, he told us he bought stock from you—but only a few shares and then no more."

"Believe me, folks," Greenleaf said in all sincerity, "I know everyone I sell to by name—in my business, you have to. And I never heard of him, at least, not by that name. Maxwell Bledsoe, you say?"

Jessie said, "He's the town's attorney, and he's also president of the local bank."

The affable swindler shook his head and laughed. "There is no way on God's green earth that I would go anywhere near either a lawyer or a bank president. It's too dangerous. In the confidence game, you work on people's greed—can't make that sale without the customer having a certain amount of avarice. But lawyers and bank presidents—and stock brokers—have an oversupply. Truth be told, they're loaded with it. And that can land you in trouble because they can get out of hand, so I steer clear of them."

Jessie said to Ki, "I thought so. I never really believed Bledsoe bought stock from an itinerate salesman. If he had, he would have showed us the certificates. Besides, swindlers"—she turned to Greenleaf—"excuse me, but that's what you are, Mr. Greenleaf, take their time in getting to know their marks, as you said."

"Then why did he recommend people buy more stock?" Archie asked.

"Yes, why?" Greenleaf chimed in.

Jessie said, "Because he knew your stock was fraudulent, that there was no such company as Henerow Corporation."

Greenleaf yelped, about to protest.

Jessie shook her head. "There isn't—I checked. And I'm sure he did, too. But he wanted people to borrow money from the bank, mortgaging their homes and property, to extend themselves far beyond their means. That way, he and the bank could foreclose on them when the stock proved worthless and they had no way to make their mortgage payments."

Graham Greenleaf grinned. "Now that's what I call a grand swindle! He talked them into buying my stock so he could get hold of their land and everything else they owned. Glory be! Call me a piker!"

"Now comes the hard part," Jessie said, smiling to soften the blow. "Please listen very carefully to what I'm about to say, because your very lives depend on getting everything straight."

Greenleaf and Archie leaned forward in their chairs, alert and ready, completely swept up in the drama unfolding before them.

Jessie continued, her somber face reflecting the seriousness of the moment. "Mr. Greenleaf—"

"Please," he interrupted, "call me Greenie. All my friends do. Or Graham—that's my first name. But"—he wrinkled his nose jovially—"Mr. Greenleaf sounds so terribly formal."

Jessie smiled again. "All right, Greenie. And you may call me Jessie. Now please pay attention and try not to interrupt. Ki and I want you to give back all the money you took from your last trip out."

150

At first stunned, both Greenleaf and Archie protested loudly, each talking over the other.

Jessie pointed out, "Look, you gentlemen have only two choices: Help us and walk away with some money, or refuse and spend a long time in prison or a very short time at the end of a rope."

The choice was clear-cut, since neither wanted to take his chances with the law. The two men agreed to help however they could.

Jessie smiled. "Good. First off, what I want you to do is to buy back all the shares of phony stock you sold to everyone in the Harcourtville area—from every last one of the people you just suckered."

The swindlers gasped.

"Plus a slight profit for your pigeons," she added, "to cover their pain and grief in having been hornswoggled out of almost everything they owned and then having nearly lost all their property."

"But—"

Jessie shook her head. "No arguments. It's our way or the law's way."

"But we've already spent some of the money," Greenie argued.

Archie shook his head. "We've gambled away most of it." He held up his coin-filled bowler. "This is it, all I got left."

"No it isn't, Arch," Greenie disagreed. "Please forgive my friend here, but he doesn't understand." He shot Archie a dirty look and continued. "We stashed most of it at Archie's shop, and I'm ahead now from poker. But I really don't think we have enough to pay everyone back and give them a profit, too."

Archie squealed and tore at his hair.

"Thank you for your candor, Greenie. And there will be no problem about having enough money, I can assure you," Ki said confidently.

Jessie further explained that she had someone she wanted to be fleeced—which is where Greenie and Archie came in—and the men could keep some of the loot. That is, they could keep all the money above and beyond what they returned to the last people Greenie sold stock to. In fact, if all went according to

151

plan, Greenie and Archie might come out with quite a profit for themselves—a possible grubstake to get them started in some honest endeavor should they choose to stay on the right side of the law.

After Jessie and Ki detailed their plans for Maxwell Bledsoe's downfall, Archie and Greenleaf returned to the print shop to make more stock certificates. It might take a day or two, since they had to wait until the ink dried. It was important for every detail to be just so this time. Their adversary, Ki and Jessie warned them, was clever and deadly—but greedy.

Jessie sent three telegrams—a fairly short one to Harcourtville; a complicated one to Wetumka; and another very lengthy, detailed one to Enid—and set the wheels in motion for their all-out attack on Maxwell Bledsoe and his band of cutthroats.

★

Chapter 22

Old Jeremiah Quincy limped his way across Harcourtville's main thoroughfare and climbed the few steps to the boarded sidewalk. The faster he tried to go, the more he puffed, his gimpy leg causing him nothing but pain and strain. The wiry little telegraph operator had been alone when the message came in for Bert and Halleybelle Harcourt, and he knew Maxwell Bledsoe would want to see it immediately.

It took Jeremiah only moments to decide to close up the telegraph office long enough to deliver such an important missive. There would be time later to send his young runner out to the Circle H Ranch to drop off the actual telegram. But it was late afternoon, and all the boys in town seemed to be somewhere else.

As he hobbled along, the elderly telegrapher wished his leg would work right—he should have called Doc Sawyer when he fell off the ladder and broke his hip. If the doc had set it properly, he reflected, he wouldn't have such a marked limp—and he wouldn't have to lie and tell everyone he'd been shot in a robbery instead of losing his balance while hanging a picture.

Michael O'Murray poked his jovial pink face out the front door of his restaurant to suck up a breath of fresh air. "Hey, Jeremiah," he called, "where you goin' in such a hurry? You'd think the wee folk was after you, the rate you're goin'." He twirled his orange mustache, not really expecting an answer from the old man.

Between puffs, Jeremiah said, "Got to see Mr. Bledsoe— very important."

"That it must be, old bucko. You couldn't move much faster if you had the bank robbers what lamed you on your tail." He laughed and returned to his customers, rubbing his hands and doing a little jig.

From across the street, Marshal Teddison watched the old telegraph operator struggling down the sidewalk. When he heard Maxwell Bledsoe's name, he brought his chair back down on all four legs and stood quickly.

"Sandy, Clint—get out here now!"

The scraggly blond wandered through the jailhouse door practicing his six-shooter spin. "What's up, Marshal? I'm busy."

"Dammit all to hell!" the marshal growled as he jammed a fresh stogie between his teeth. "You don't get paid to play with your revolver, you—"

Clint rushed out past Sandy, an eager look on his acned face. "You need more cigars, Marshal?" He stopped short when he saw the lawman's new stogie protruding from the back of his jaw. "I'm here. What's the hurry?"

The town marshal squinted at his deputies. "Jeremiah Quincy just passed by on his way to Maxwell Bledsoe's office—with a telegram. Let's save the boss a little time and get there before he sends Spike to fetch us."

The three lawmen fell into step, heading for Maxwell Bledsoe's law offices. In the minutes it took to gather his deputies, Marshal Teddison had lost sight of Jeremiah Quincy. The old man had disappeared, and there seemed no doubt he had already presented the telegram to Bledsoe.

The marshal shook his head. "Iffen I'd've thought about it, I should've sent one of you fellas to stay at the telegraph office. That way, we coulda gotten the jump on Mr. Bledsoe."

Clint picked at a massive pimple on his cheek. "What good would that do? He's gonna tell us what's in it now anyway, ain't he?"

"Yeah," the marshal mumbled, "but we're supposed to be better than Spike and his gang. I just wished we coulda proved it."

"We will," Sandy said as they reached the law offices and climbed the steep wooden staircase.

Marshal Teddison took the steps two at a time, reaching the office door long before his lethargic deputies. "Oh, for crissakes, get the lead out!" He turned and barged into the reception room.

"Hello there, Marshal," Violet Davis said in greeting, her peaches-and-cream complexion as radiant as ever. "What can I do for you today?"

"I wanna see Maxwell, of course." The marshal eyed the light-haired receptionist suspiciously. "Is Jeremiah Quincy still with him?"

Violet adjusted her bustle and blinked at the lawman. "No. In fact, I haven't seen old Jeremiah is several days. Did you forget? This is Friday, Marshal—and you should know Mr. B is always at the bank on Fridays." She giggled softly and batted her lashes at Sandy, who stood just behind the marshal. "There hasn't been a Friday in years that he hasn't been at the bank. Now why in the world would you think he was here?"

Without a word, Marshal Teddison left the comely spinster receptionist still going on about her employer's comings and goings. He took the stairs three at a time going down and rushed out onto the sidewalk. Off in the distance, over a block away, he saw Jeremiah Quincy limping his way back to the telegraph office.

"Dammit all to hell! I missed 'im!" The marshal bit down and ripped off the end of his stogie.

The deputies, who had just reached the sidewalk, looked at each other, trying to understand why the marshal would be so upset. They shrugged their shoulders at each other and fell in behind him.

"Hurry up—let's get there before Spike comes looking for us."

Marshal Teddison took off at a trot, the two men half his age trying desperately to keep up with him. When he reached the front door to the bank, he stopped to catch his breath, and his deputies collided with him, running up his back. He hit Clint with his ten-gallon hat and leaned against the doorway while he lighted what was left of the stogie. Then he casually entered the bank and approached Hiram Abernathy, the head clerk.

"Good afternoon, Hiram. We're here to see Mr. Bledsoe." The marshal looked around for Spike. "We'll let ourselves in if that's all right with you."

"Yes, sir—of course, sir," Hiram stammered, his ears turning pink.

As Marshal Teddison's hand closed around the doorknob to Bledsoe's office, the door jerked open, pulling the marshal in with it. His deputies tried unsuccessfully to stifle their laughter as Spike lumbered through the door.

"Sorry, Marshal," Spike said. "I was just on my way to find you. Pretty good timing, huh?"

The lawman caught his balance and sauntered into the office. He glanced at the piece of paper in Bledsoe's hand and smiled. "Well, Maxwell, I see you got a telegram. Is it from that Starbuck girl?"

"It most certainly is!" He motioned for Hiram Abernathy, who ran to the doorway. "Hiram, I'll be with Marshal Teddison. Please see that we are not disturbed."

"Oh, yes, sir, I will." The young man ushered the deputies and Spike out the door and closed it behind them. "Please wait here," he said, pointing to a reception area beside his desk.

As soon as the door closed, Maxwell Bledsoe handed the marshal the telegram. "They are alive, just as I suspected. And they're coming back to help the Harcourts, just as I knew they would."

Marshal Teddison read the wire and handed it back. "I wonder what they're doing in Wichita. At least they didn't get to Oklahoma City or Wetumka, which means they probably haven't caught up with Graham Greenleaf yet." He tossed the stub of his stogie into the nearest cuspidor. "Let's see now, from Wichita, they'll more than likely take the stagecoach straight here, crossing the great salt plains." He rubbed his hands together. "And we'll ambush them at the caverns. We can lay in wait for as long as it takes, and the driver won't see us until he's right on top of us and it's too late. That should be that."

Maxwell Bledsoe beamed at the town marshal and reached for his meerschaum and some tobacco. "Damn good, Marshal. No one could accuse us of anything if some *banditos* hold up the stagecoach and massacre the passengers and drivers. No witnesses, no problems."

The marshal picked up the telegram again. "It says here that they're leaving Wichita tomorrow—stage doesn't leave until then." He pulled another cigar from his pocket, crinkled it in his hands and sniffed it. Sucking on the tip, he clenched it between his teeth. "Well, I'll get the boys ready and we'll ride on out tonight. Barring any screw-ups, we should get to the caverns long before they do."

Silvery muttonchops bristling with pleasure, Maxwell Bledsoe grinned at the lawman. He picked up a copy of the *New York Times* and waved the front page at the marshal. "See this? If you and your men are successful, I'll be making headlines in this paper sooner than you'd think." He stared at the front page, his voice drifting. "Maxwell Bledsoe, governor and founder of the state of Bledsoe, throws his hat into the ring—the first presidential candidate from west of the Mississippi."

The marshal leaned over as if reading the front page. "Does it say anything there about Lieutenant Governor Teddison?"

★
Chapter 23

The success of the plan to undo Maxwell Bledsoe lay squarely in Graham Greenleaf's trustworthiness. Jessie and Ki knew that if Greenie took off with the spoils from his last venture in Harcourt County, all would be lost. If they could stay with the confidence man, they might be able to ensure his steadfastness, but each of the four played different roles and had to be in separate locations.

"Do you think we can trust him?" Ki asked one last time as he paced the hotel suite living room.

"His candor when Archie lied about how much money they had left over tells us something. He may not be completely trustworthy, but he does have principles. In some ways, I think he's ethical." Jessie chuckled heartily. "And I think he's enjoying himself. There's nothing a swindler loves more than a challenge—except a chance to swindler another swindler."

Ki nodded. "You're right. We've provided him with both, and he has every opportunity to become quite wealthy. I guess my only worry is Archie MacTaggert. Every chain has a weak link, and he's ours."

"I agree. He's a man of more larceny than ethics—a total lack of integrity. I just hope Greenie can keep him in line." Jessie brushed an errant blond curl from her forehead. "Of course, stipulating that Greenie was to be in charge of the money helps the situation. If Archie should choose to leave or try to foul things up, he gets no money." She looked around the room. "All right, I'm ready to go—how about you?"

"I've been waiting on you," Ki replied. "Let's hit the road— we wouldn't want to be late to our own massacre, now would we?"

The pair laughed as they vacated the 'presidential suite.' Jessie had arranged for a special Concord to replace the usual mud wagon that carried passengers and mail between Wichita and Harcourtville. More comfortable and enclosed, the sturdy Concord would also make better time and offer better protection from raids and attacks.

Thurmond and his assistant Aaron greeted Jessie and Ki at the hotel steps. The special Concord, shining and spotless, waited out front. As Thurmond helped Jessie up into the customized stagecoach, Ki handed Aaron their gear and saddles, which the young assistant driver stowed in the boot. Once Ki settled himself in the carriage next to Jessie, and Thurmond and Aaron yelled at the team, they sped off on the first leg of their adventure.

Sitting atop the Concord, Thurmond said, "You know, Aaron, you're damn lucky to be my assistant. For years I've been hearing about Jessica Starbuck and her companion Ki, and now we get to meet them. But not just meet 'em— we get to work for 'em! Can you beat that?"

Bright-eyed and impressionable, young Aaron nodded. "I can hardly believe it! I jes' hope I do everythin' jes' right. I'd hate to be the one to toss a brandin' iron into the fire!"

"Don't worry, kid, you'll do just fine. You've played cowboys and Indians 'afore, ain't you? Well, that's all there is to it. I don't know no kid what cain't die convincingly. We all done it as youngsters—now we get to do it again." He grinned a yellow grin and slapped the lead horses with the reins, picking up more speed.

"Golly, that Miss Starbuck sure must be rich—buying this Concord from the stagecoach line—and us to go with it! What a darn shame it'd be iffen the stagecoach gets wrecked or burned, but she don't seem to care none."

Thurmond smiled. "That's the whole point. With what she's got planned, she don't want the coach line to lose

160

money from it. Damn, I can hardly wait!"

Inside the carriage, Jessie and Ki went over the plans once again, fully aware that everything had to go just right or it would all fall apart.

Graham Greenleaf opened the bulging carpetbag for the bank president to see. "I want to open a new account and deposit all this in it. I also have a letter of credit from Jessica Starbuck at the First Bank of Austin to cover any and all checks I may write on the account."

Miles Bedecker, president of the Oklahoma City Bank and Trust, stared at the mass of coins and paper money—and then at the letter of credit, not sure whether he was more impressed with the amount of cash before him or the letter of credit from an empire so vast it was legendary.

"I can't thank you enough for bringing your business to our humble institution." Miles, who at fifty-two thought he had seen everything, hoped he wasn't groveling but felt impelled to rattle on. "I'm sorry, but it will take several days to a week or more to get your bank drafts printed for you under the Henerow Corporation heading. In the meantime, Mr. Greenleaf, we'll be very happy to honor any paper with your signature on it until further notice."

"Thank you. My company and I appreciate this, but I've already had my own bank drafts printed up with the company monogram and all." He withdrew one from his inside breast pocket and offered it to the bank president. When Miles handed the draft back to Greenleaf, he wrote *void* across it and handed it back to the bank official. "Please show this to your employees—they will be the only checks to be written on this account."

From the bank, the confidence man headed for the telegraph office. If the message he'd been waiting for was there, he would be on his way. His pulse quickened as he approached the office. It seemed difficult to understand that something as legal as this could produce the same thrill of the chase as his most illegal confidence games.

As Greenleaf stepped through the narrow doorway into the small office, the tapping key told him this was definitely the right place. The hollow clackety-clack of metal on metal meant news for someone—good news for him, he hoped. He approached the counter and waited for the telegrapher to finish taking down the incoming message. Two young boys sat next to the desk with legs sprawled, obviously waiting to run the wire to its destination.

When the lumpy telegrapher put down his pencil and folded the piece of paper, the larger of the two boys jumped up and grabbed it from the man's hand. The man looked out from under his green visor and smiled, then glanced at Greenleaf, seeing him for the first time.

"Be with you in just a moment, young man," he said, tidying up his desk. "Now, what can I do you for?" he said playfully.

Greenleaf smiled at being called a young man. "My name is Graham Greenleaf. Are there any messages for me? I'm expecting at least one—maybe two."

"Greenleaf, Greenleaf—now that's sounds familiar." The telegrapher scratched his fuzzy bald head and searched the office with his eyes. "Seems to me I got a wire just an hour or so ago." He tugged at the black garter on each sleeve of his off white muslin shirt. "Yup, I was right—here they be, two of 'em. One of 'em came in late yesterday." As he handed the telegrams over to Greenleaf, he scratched his bristly gray beard.

The dapper confidence man unfolded the first telegram and read it quickly. Good! Archie finished his part of it, and it's on its way. Now, he thought, all I have to do is meet the train, and we're all set. "Thank you," he called out as he left the telegraph office and headed for the train station at a fast pace. The sooner he picked it up, the sooner he'd be on his way to Harcourtville and the showdown.

He casually opened the other telegram, knowing it had to be from Jessica and Ki. As he walked along, he read the short wire telling him that another letter of credit drawn on the Bank of Austin would be waiting for him when he got to Harcourtville—to be used only if he really needed it. His chest swelled with pride—they trusted him! Letters of credit were like gold, and he had two of them from one of the wealthiest people on earth . . . who trusted him. He would make every effort to see that her trust was well placed.

★

Chapter 24

Marshal Teddison and his eight deputies waited at the great salt plains caverns. The stagecoach from Wichita carrying Jessica Starbuck and her Chinaman would be along in a few minutes, the marshal pointed out, and he sent Zack Bartlett to act as lookout. Zack climbed to the top of the hill above the caverns to keep a watch and would whistle when the carriage came into view from a mile off around the bend.

Sandy pouted and said, "How come you're takin' Clint with you to stop the coach, Marshal? Why not me?"

"Cuz you look too mean. If I'm gonna get close enough to them to get the drop on 'em, I gotta make sure they don't suspect nothin'. Clint looks harmless enough, but you don't. Got that?"

Sandy ran his fingers through his poor imitation of a beard and thought about it. "Well, the two of you ain't gonna be able to kill the driver and the guard and all the passengers, too, not all by yourselves."

The marshal shook his head. "I already told you and the rest—we're gonna stop the coach and warn 'em that Injuns are on the warpath." He chomped on his unlit stogie and pushed his ten-gallon hat way back. "They won't suspect nothin', what with me being town marshal and all. Once I got the stagecoach stopped, then all the rest of you come out Remingtons blazing." He smiled and held up his hands. "That way, Clint and I only

163

have to take care of one each." He looked each man in the face. "Now, you all got that straight or do I have to go over it again?"

The deputies shook their heads.

Slick laughed. "And then we make it look like it was stagecoach robbers what done it."

Suddenly, Zack's whistle sounded from above. Twice he let loose with a shrill call, and Marshall Teddison and Clint mounted up.

"All right, now," the marshal yelled, "remember not to shoot until me and Clint's got the damn coach to a full stop. I'll shoot the lead horse, so the coach can't go nowheres. Then you come out shootin'. And watch what yer doin' and don't shoot us. Got that?"

The men nodded as the marshal and his pimply-faced deputy headed their steeds to the entrance of the caverns. Just as they reached the opening, they heard shots—dozens of rifle shots coming from down the road and around the bend. Warily, they peeked out to the road, but could see nothing. The gunfire continued, a steady round after round—and then they heard war whoops, Indian war cries.

Marshal Teddison and Clint dismounted and scrambled up the side of the cavern to where Zack sat watching the road. A half-mile down, dozens of painted Cherokee warriors circled the stagecoach, firing into the air and terrorizing the drivers and passengers.

The driver tried to outrun the Indians, but when a brave jumped on the lead horse, the stagecoach came to an abrupt halt. The driver and the stage guard raised their hands in surrender.

"By God, this is just what we needed!" the marshal cried. "Those renegades are doing our job for us! Look!" He pointed as if no one else had seen the bloodcurdling drama being played out off in the distance.

"Jeez," Zack muttered, "I wouldn't wanna be in their boots right now. It's one thing for us to shoot 'em dead, but to be killed by Injuns . . . jeez!"

The rest of Teddison's deputies scurried up to the vantage point to see what the noise was all about. As the men watched, the stagecoach driver and guard threw down their weapons and raised their hands high again. Several braves, their bodies covered in full war paint, still circled the coach, discharging their rifles. Some of the braves jumped on the team of horses and undid the harnesses. It appeared obvious the Indians planned to take the horses with them as part of the plunder.

Some warriors boarded the coach, and the lawmen could hear shouts and screams coming from inside the carriage as the driver and his assistant shouted for the braves to stop but were thrown from the driver's seat. Suddenly, a Cherokee brave climbed out of the carriage with a blond woman in a light green frock and a bonnet over his shoulder. She screamed and pounded on him, but he ran to a warrior on a painted pony and handed the struggling blonde up. The brave with three feathers in his hair galloped off with her slung over his pony in front of him.

Another Cherokee hauled a limp body from the carriage and helped hand the tall man with long black hair up onto a second horse. As the brave rode away, two more rode up and grabbed the stagecoach driver and guard off the ground where they sat sprawled and threw them over the front of their horses and took off. Finally, two braves dragged the last passenger yelling and kicking off the stagecoach and up onto a horse. The bald man kept hitting his captor on the head with his bowler.

Before the brave carrying a torch set fire to the stagecoach, several warriors removed everything from the boot and handed it up to mounted braves. The last of the Cherokee renegades circled and shot off their rifles until the coach flamed into a ball of fire and burned to the ground. Whooping and yelling, the raiding party rode south to catch up with the braves and their prisoners.

"If that don't beat all!" Marshal Teddison said as the Cherokee warriors galloped out of view. "This sure was their unlucky day, and that's a fact! Iffen those renegades hadn't got them, we woulda."

The men laughed till they nearly cried. What a joke. Slapping and nudging one another, they found it hard to stop from laughing.

Sandy suddenly sobered up and blew his nose on his neck-erchief. "Damn! They did our job for us—and we didn't have no fun! I was kinda lookin' forward to it."

Mule-eyed Luke snorted as he laughed and wiped tears from his cheeks. "Oh, fer crissakes, Sandy, you dimwit. Thems the magic words—they done the job for us! Get it? Now we kin go back and tell Mr. Bledsoe we done the job, and maybe get a bonus for burning the coach and making it look like Injuns done it!"

Everyone laughed as the marshal nodded. "Goddamn it all to hell, Luke, you ain't got too much upstairs, but when you get a good idea, you shore make it a doozy!" He banged Luke on the back and shook his hand. "That's it, fellas, that's what we're gonna do. I'll tell Maxwell that we staged a phony Injun raid and burned the carriage to the ground and buried the bodies off in the salt flats where nobody'll ever find their bones but prairie dogs and gophers."

Before heading back to town, the lawmen rode out to where the remnants of the stagecoach smoldered in the dust. They poked through the embers and rubble, but found nothing. The Indians had obviously picked it clean. Marshal Teddison got off his horse and inspected the Indian ponies' hoofmarks—no shoes. Satisfied, he mounted up and motioned everyone to follow him west.

As the marshal and his deputies rode toward town to report on their success, back at the Cherokee settlement north of Waynoka, Jessie and Ki thanked Chief Running Buffalo and his warriors for staging the raid.

Jessie signed to the chief and his people, "Now the debt you feel you owed us for saving little Raging River is paid in full." She shook the chief's hand and hugged the papoose whose life she had saved.

Running Buffalo signed and spoke through Ki, "Golden Eagle very wise to send message to Running Buffalo over white man's wire at Waynoka. Telegraph man say he never before have such long message. But your instructions good, and we glad to help. Only sorry to burn beautiful stagecoach." He smiled and gave a short chuckle. "Thank you—it was much fun. We do it again sometime?"

Ki laughed. "I hope not. But with Golden Eagle, one never knows."

Jessie shook her head. "Please don't worry about the stagecoach, Chief. It was very old and about to be torn apart anyway. I bought it for very little and it more than served its purpose." She gazed at all her new friends and said a personal good-bye to each before ducking into one of the huts to change into her riding clothes.

Ki and Jessie waved one last time as they mounted up on two of the team horses, all of which were riding horses. Their saddles were part of the plunder the Cherokee braves took from the boot.

Almost before the marshal and his deputies reached Harcourtville, having stopped off to celebrate with some well-deserved suds on their way back, Jessie and Ki arrived at the Circle H Ranch. Archie MacTaggert, the stagecoach's third passenger, set off by wagon for Harcourtville to complete his part of the plan while Thurmond and Aaron returned to the stagecoach line via Waynoka.

★
Chapter 25

Dapper as ever in his fancy brown frock coat and vest, Graham Greenleaf knocked on Amanda Hammond's front door. The sixty-year-old's big blue eyes lighted up when she swung open the massive door to find Greenleaf standing on the stoop. Her first reaction was to run to the boudoir to fix herself up, since she had not expected guests. She yanked off her muslin apron and stuffed it into a drawer of the hall credenza and straightened her hair. She realized there was nothing she could do about her tattered gingham dress and filthy old work shoes.

"No, please, Widow Hammond, don't go to any bother. You always look lovely to me. Besides, this is not a social call—I'm here on the most serious business."

"Oh, my! I heard something about the stock not being any good. So it's true after all? I defended you to everyone, you know—told them all you were no thief." Her face clouded and her lower lip pouted out.

Greenleaf shook his head. "Oh, no! I appreciate your faith in me, my dear woman, and it is a happy visit that I make. I am here to buy back all the stock you bought from me."

Confusion mixed with her initial disappointment. "But I don't understand. If you're supposed to be a fraud, why would you want to give me my money back?"

The swindler laughed. "Amanda, my lovely, I am not a fraud," he said with a perfectly straight face, the same face he used to bluff so well in poker. "In fact, I am not only going to buy back your stock, but I am also going to pay you a dividend for each share at ten percent over what you paid me. That means that for every dollar you paid, I will pay you one dollar and ten cents. But I must have the stock certificates back—you do still have them, don't you?"

"Of course I do. They're so pretty, even when everyone said they were worthless, I still kept them." She went to the settee in the living room and sat down hard. "I can't believe this is happening—it's like Christmas!"

Greenleaf sat opposite her and laughed. "Well, merry Christmas and happy birthday, Amanda, my pet. I've come to buy back your stock. Run get me the certificates, and I'll write you a bank draft as good as cash—better even, truth be told."

The woman shook her salt-and-pepper curls. "A bank draft? I don't know . . . "

"I tell you what, my dear. You count up your certificates for me, and I'll write out the bank draft." His kindly hazel eyes soothed her apprehension. "You can take the draft to the bank in Harcourtville right now and cash it. If it's no good, you're out nothing but an hour of your time. But if the bank cashes the draft and gives you the money, then I'll take the certificates. Is that fair enough?"

Her eyes wide in amazement, she stammered, "I-I guess it is. In fact, now you're going to have to trust me, aren't you? After all, I could keep your cash and the certificates, too."

Greenleaf's laugh bounced off the walls. "My dear Amanda, what a refreshing sense of humor. I would never believe that you could cheat me, any more than you thought it of me." He pulled out his Waltham and listened to make sure it was working. "I must run now, there are so many more people to see." He stopped as if pondering. "Listen, I have an idea. I'm headed for Harcourtville right now, truth be told. The people I have to see are just on the other side of town."

"Oh?" Her eyes sparkled with anticipation.

"Perhaps I could give you a ride to town in my buckboard. While you're at the bank, I could be visiting my next customer. When I'm done there, I could pick you up and return you here. How does that sound?"

"Delightful, perfectly delightful! I presume the bank will have to telegraph your bank anyway, and that will take time. So you might be ready even before I am." She jumped up and ran to the foyer. "Please give me a minute to change my frock and run a brush through my hair. I won't be long, really I won't."

Greenleaf watched her disappear into another room, probably the boudoir. He smiled to himself—the first stage of the plan had worked perfectly, and there was no reason to believe that the next step would go any less smoothly. Ah, he reflected, if only Miss Starbuck would join forces with me! He felt sure they would make a marvelous confidence team. His agile mind created a delicious swindle.

Jessie and Ki slipped into the Harcourt mansion through the back entrance, having gotten off and walked their horses for at least a quarter-mile. There was little time to chat, since the plan was in motion. Bert told Jessie and Ki of Maxwell Bledsoe's massive foreclosures, and Jessie explained their plan at great length.

Bert said, "I went into town and spoke with Mike over at Mom's Grub Shop. He's game and wants to help out, just as you suggested. It's almost unbelievable that Bledsoe would read our telegrams, but he must have—that's the only way Marshal Teddison and his deputies would know when you planned to arrive."

Jessie smiled. "Believe me, I counted on that."

"We've also spoken with all the people Graham Greenleaf sold stock to," Halleybelle said. "There's nothing any of them would rather do than get back at lawyer Bledsoe. He's made life a living hell here in Harcourt County. The sooner he's behind bars, the better."

Bert disagreed. "Hanging's too good for him! I'd like to shoot him right between the eyes and dance on his grave! Imagine, foreclosing on the Baumgartners and their eleven youngsters."

"I think you'll find this equally as delicious a revenge," Jessie said. "We're hitting him where he lives—right in the old pocketbook." She laughed. "Now, remember, when he shows up at your door, don't sell the stock for less than a dollar fifty on the dollar. Depending on how he reacts, you might push it up to two."

"Have there been any further raids on this ranch?" Ki asked.

"No, but Halleybelle is still quite shaky," Bert said. "If they hurt her, I'll personally wipe them all out! With my bare hands!"

"Bert, stop it!" his sister said. "Let's forget that for the moment and concentrate on bleeding Bledsoe."

Jessie, Ki and Bert looked at Halleybelle, laughing at her unintended pun. They all reflected that a good hearty laugh helped relieve the tension.

Archie MacTaggert pulled his buckboard up outside Mom's Grub Shop and hitched the reins. He sauntered in casually and looked around to see who was there before sitting at the counter. When Mike approached, wiping his face on his stained apron, Archie nodded and put a copy of the *New York Times* on the counter in front of him.

"Have you seen my friend Graham Greenleaf lately?" Archie asked conversationally.

Mike looked over at the customers at a table by the window and the deputy seated at the other end of the counter and winked at Archie. "Nope, ain't seen him in the longest time—that good-for-nothin' swindler."

Archie shook his head and laughed. "That's what everyone thought," he said loud enough for all to hear without appearing to, "but it turns out Greenie's gettin' the last laugh." He opened the newspaper and pointed to an article on the lower half of the front page continued on the inside. "Just read that and see who's the swindler."

Mike picked up the paper and read aloud: "Wetumka, Oklahoma Territory. One of the biggest gushers in the history of the petroleum business came in last week, Henerow Corporation announced at its annual board meeting in New York City today." Mike whistled. "Now, that's something!"

"Read on," Archie encouraged.

"Samuel A. Kurrle, president and chief executive officer of Henerow Corporation, stated at the board meeting that the news of the gusher had purposely been kept under wraps until the extent of the venture could be ascertained." Mike frowned. "Why, those dirty dogs! By doin' that, they made everybody think Mr. Greenleaf was a confidence man."

Archie lowered his voice to a stage whisper. "From what I hear, Greenie is trying to buy back as much of the stock as he can before anyone finds out what their stock is really worth. Now that the value has skyrocketed, iffen he can get it all back, he'll be a multimillionaire. Thank goodness he was my buddy—I believed in him and bought a whole bunch of shares. I'm on my way to being filthy rich myself! Thank God nobody out West reads the *New York Times* or everybody'd know about this." He folded the paper and shoved it into his pocket.

The deputy finished his stew and coffee, plunked down a coin, and ran out the door toward the jailhouse. The customers by the window also left in a hurry without finishing their food. As soon as they were alone, Archie and Mike smirked but held back the delicious guffaw they both wanted to enjoy. The plan was working.

Slick ran as hard as he could across the street, bursting into the jailhouse with a holler. "Where's the marshal! I gotta talk to him right now!"

Sandy looked up from his six-shooter spinning practice. "What's the big rush? He's over at the bank with Mr. Bledsoe. Probably still tellin' him about the Injun raid we 'fixed up' for the stagecoach." He went back to spinning the revolver, first in one hand, then in the other.

Slick dashed out the door and down the street to the bank. He rushed past Hiram Abernathy and into Bledsoe's office without so much as a knock. The bank president and the town marshal looked startled as Slick barged in. They had been in the middle of a toast, holding their brandy snifters up high.

"What the hell!" Bledsoe cried. "Where do you get the nerve to come racing in here without even knocking?"

The marshal said, "Slick, what's gotten into you? Is something wrong?"

"Nope! Something's really right! You know them stock shares everybody's been so het up about? Well, the gusher came in!"

"Ridiculous! Preposterous!" Bledsoe muttered. "Marshal, are all your deputies this weak-witted?"

Slick shook his head. "No, it's true—I swear. If you had a copy of the *New York Times*, you could see for yourself. A guy over at the grub shop had a copy, and he told Mike. I was there—I heard!"

"The mail from Oklahoma City just arrived," Bledsoe said. "In fact, Hiram probably has it out on his desk right now. Slick, tell Hiram to bring me the mail."

The deputy rushed for the door and called to Hiram to bring in Mr. Bledsoe's mail. In moments, the week's mail was on Bledsoe's desk.

Leafing through the paper, the bank president said, "Well? Where the hell is it? You said it was here, but I don't see it."

Slick pointed to the lower part of the first page, and grinned with pride. "See, I told you so!"

Bledsoe read it aloud for Marshal Teddison. The two stared at each other and took a large gulp of brandy. Both men lighted up—the marshal, his stogie, and Bledsoe, his pipe.

"Oh, my God! If anyone gets wind of this, I'm ruined! All those people I encouraged to buy more and more shares—they're rich as Midas." He took another long pull on his brandy and thought for a moment. "But, wait . . . "

"Yeah?" the marshal said. "What do you have up your sleeve?"

Bledsoe looked over at the deputy. "Thank you very much, Slick. I won't forget this. Now, please let us have a little privacy."

As Slick left, Hiram knocked at the door. "Sir, Mrs. Hammond is here with a bank draft for twenty thousand dollars. She wants to know if we can cash it for her."

"Let me see the draft." He reached out for it and saw what he had hoped not to see—it was made out from Henerow Corporation. "Oh, my God!" He motioned Hiram out. "Close the door, please. I'll speak with you in a moment. Ask Mrs. Hammond to wait."

The marshal looked puzzled. "What's the problem? Does it have anything to do with the stock certificates?"

"Damn it all to hell, it most certainly does! From the looks of this, Greenleaf is using his inside knowledge to buy back all the stock. He'll make a fortune if he gets away with it."

"But I thought there was no such company—isn't that what you said before?"

"For crissakes," Bledsoe said, holding up the newspaper, "do you think the *Times* would lie?"

"No, but—"

"Oh, shut up! I've got to think." He puffed on his cherrywood pipe and drummed his fingers on the desk. "Aha! I have it! I have it! I'll buy back the stock before Greenleaf gets to them, starting with Mrs. Hammond." He jumped up, rushed out to the lobby, bank draft in hand, and ushered the widow into his office. He said good-bye to the marshal and ushered him out.

Mrs. Hammond looked apprehensive as he closed the door. "Is the draft all right? Will the bank cash it?"

"Of course, it's all right." He had to tell the truth about that, he thought to himself, just in case someone checked later. "But I think you're being cheated. I happen to know that the price of the stock went up by fifteen percent. How much above retail is he paying you?"

"Ten percent."

"There, you see? He's making a profit off you. That is most unprincipled—not the gentlemanly thing to do. Now, remember, Amanda, I was the one who recommended you buy more stock. I want to be the one to buy it from you at a decent profit . . . say, twenty percent?"

"Why, Maxwell Bledsoe, that's terribly sweet of you, but I couldn't let you do that. I have the certificates right here, and I'll just take the money from the draft and be done with it."

"All right, I'll pay you twenty-five percent. How does that sound?"

She smiled, her blue eyes shining. "Oh, my. I never really promised him, now did I?" She dug into her large bag and retrieved the stock certificates. "Cash," she asked, "or will you deposit to my account?"

Bledsoe handed her back the bank draft and accepted the stock certificates. He rang for Hiram, who rushed in. "Please

175

credit Mrs. Hammond's account with a dollar and a quarter per certificate. And keep this quiet. Take the funds from my account—this is a personal transaction. I'll sign the necessary papers when you have them ready."

Half an hour later, Graham Greenleaf picked up Amanda Hammond outside the bank. On the way back to her house, she explained to him what had happened. She had expected Mr. Greenleaf to be extremely put out with her, but as the true gentleman she knew him to be, he accepted her news with only mild chagrin. In fact, if she didn't know better, she could have sworn he was smiling.

★

Chapter 26

After Maxwell Bledsoe telegraphed Oklahoma City to assure himself that the Henerow Corporation bank draft was indeed good and that the account it was drawn on had enough funds to buy and sell his bank, the bank president prepared to visit each of Greenleaf's customers and outbid him. But an even easier method of obtaining the Henerow shares presented itself.

A second customer came to the bank wanting to know if the Henerow bank draft he had was good. Bledsoe invited the bearer into his office and offered him more than Greenleaf had offered. The customer agreed, no questions asked, and handed over the certificates he had with him.

Bledsoe realized that he could let Greenleaf do all his work for him. Let Greenleaf send the customer into the bank with his certificates and the bank draft, and he'd do his outbidding right in the office. With the price of the shares going up steadily, by the time he had his hands on all the stock, he could buy half the West. In no time at all, he mused, he would have his own republic.

Bert and Halleybelle Harcourt asked Hiram Abernathy to see if the bank draft they had would be good. Again, the young man brought the draft to Mr. Bledsoe, who invited the Harcourt brother and sister into his office.

"Please be seated, won't you? Before addressing the issue of the bank draft, I want to tell you just how badly I feel about what's gone on over the mortgage. If there had been any way I could have forestalled a foreclosure, I would have—after all, you two have been very close to my heart. Your grandfather was my dearest friend, you know."

Bert and Halleybelle sat quietly, enduring the pap the man handed them. Inside, they thrilled to hear his excuses and his attempt to weasel out of everything. But they dared not show their emotions. They both stared at him blankly.

"Now, as to your bank draft here. It's good, yes, indeed it is. But I notice it's drawn on a Henerow Corporation account. If that's the same oil company stock I recommended your grandmother buy, I would very much like to buy it from you. It's the least I can do for Harold and Esmeralda's grandchildren."

The man's smile nearly made the brother and sister ill, but they swallowed hard and kept their emotions in check—for the moment.

"Thank you, Mr. Bledsoe," Halleybelle said softly, her auburn hair framing her creamy complexion, "but I think we're making enough of a profit off Mr. Greenleaf. We wouldn't want to take advantage of you, now would we, Bert?"

"Nope. That just wouldn't be the Christian thing to do. At first I was against even a fifteen percent profit, but when he upped it to twenty-five and then thirty percent, I knew I had to bend."

The bank president gulped and lighted his meerschaum pipe, drawing on it slowly, trying to keep himself calm. The price seemed to be going up, but this, too, could be weathered if handled properly.

"Considering what my bank has put you through"—the words *my bank* sent a chill through the grandchildren of the bank's founder—"the least I can do is to buy the stock from you at a fair profit. The anguish of possibly losing everything your grandfather built up, that's worth money, and I feel I should bear the burden. Please. It would make me feel much better."

Bert and Halleybelle looked at each other as if asking what to do.

Seeing doubt on their faces, Bledsoe pounced. "Tell you what, I'll pay you one-and-a-half times the price of the certificates. I can't be much fairer than that, now can I?" His gaze caught the hesitation in their concentration. I must be getting close to their price, he thought. "Well, perhaps I was being a little too conservative." He smiled expansively. "How does double the price of your stock sound? Just because you're Harcourts."

Halleybelle turned to Bert. "Please, Bert. Twice what we paid for it? That's a lot of money! Oh, please don't turn it down. We can meet the mortgage payments with it."

Bert sat there and stared into space. He hoped his face wouldn't betray him, so he counted to fifty slowly just to keep his face a blank and Bledsoe waiting. Finally, he said, "I guess if I don't take it, I'll never hear the end of it, will I?" He held out his hands. "All right, Mr. Bledsoe, it's a deal."

Bledsoe nearly shouted with joy. There were very few shares still out, and he had amassed them all. After having paid double to the Harcourts, he would probably have to pay that to the others as well. But it would be worth it, considering what the *Times* said the stock was doing. He would have it all within a day or so; then he could sit on it and wait until it had quadrupled in price. Then he'd sell.

As the Harcourts left, Hiram knocked gently on the door. "May I speak with you, sir? I have been crediting all these people's accounts with the funds from your account. But your account is now empty. What do I do? The Harcourts want to have the money credited to their account, and there isn't enough there. Please tell me what to do."

"No problem." Bledsoe pulled at his silvery muttonchops. "I'll take care of it Monday morning. Just credit the bank's funds to the Harcourts' account for the weekend. I have more cash at home, and I can raise still more by Monday."

The last customer showed up on Friday. Clarence Baumgartner, with certificates in a big bag, wanted to cash the Henerow Corporation bank draft. He had been paid two-and-a-half times what he'd paid for the stock. Bledsoe quickly upped the offer to three times its price and had Hiram credit the account.

Finally, the moment he had been waiting for arrived, when Graham Greenleaf himself walked into the bank and demanded to see Maxwell Bledsoe. Hiram ushered the dapper confidence man into the president's office and slipped away to his desk.

"Well, my good man, so we finally meet," Bledsoe said affably. "I hear you're trying to buy up all the stock you sold. But now you're out of customers. I have them all—all the certificates you originally sold." His grin sparkled with pleasure.

Greenleaf cleared his throat hesitantly, offering the bank president the picture of a cornered man. "Sir, I know what you've been doing, and I'm here to buy up the stock from you. Why would you want worthless stock? I admit it was a scheme to bilk innocent people of their money. The least I can do before I join the seminary is to buy back the fraudulent shares you're stuck with."

Bledsoe laughed from the belly, his dark brown eyes dancing merrily. "Oh, you're good! You're very, very good, my man. But never try to bamboozle a bamboozler." He lighted up his pipe and puffed. "Now, I'll tell you what I'm going to do. I'm going to do you a favor and buy up all the certificates you still have left—assuming you have any left to sell."

"You'll what?"

"You heard me right. I'll pay you what I've been paying the others. Otherwise, I just might call the territorial authorities and see what you're wanted for."

Greenleaf put up a valiant fight before finally allowing Bledsoe to win and buy the stock he had left over. Greenleaf sold the bank president every last certificate Archie had printed, and demanded cash.

Bledsoe called Hiram in and asked him to fill Greenleaf's carpetbag with the amount written on the piece of paper he slipped to the young clerk. The clerk's eyes bugged wide, and he almost refused. But he decided his employer must know what he was doing, so Hiram did as he was bid. When he'd filled the bag, be lugged it back to the office.

Greenleaf smiled. "I tell you what, Bledsoe, old man. How about if I buy you a drink or two at the saloon? I'll leave my bag here till we get back, if that's all right with you."

Pleased with himself, the bank president agreed and the two left for a celebration. While they drank and laughed and exchanged anecdotes, Hiram was left in charge. Bledsoe knew he didn't have to be back until at least two in the afternoon, and it was barely noon. He sipped his whiskey and enjoyed the sweetness of victory over the vanquished.

When Greenleaf pulled out his Waltham to check the time, it was exactly two. "I'd better be going now," he said. "I'll walk you back to the bank and pick up my money."

"No hard feelings?" Bledsoe asked.

"None whatsoever."

As they entered the bank, Hiram rushed over to Bledsoe and asked to speak to him in his office. Graham Greenleaf picked up his carpetbag and walked out of the bank, leaning to the right from the weight of the bag.

"All right, Abernathy, what it so important?"

"Well, sir, I don't rightly know where to begin. First off, everyone whose accounts you credited money to came in while you were out and withdrew all the money in cash. The bank has no more funds!"

Bledsoe glowered. "What do you mean—first off! What could be worse than that?"

Hiram swallowed hard and squinted as if ready to duck. "The bank examiner is here from Oklahoma City to see the books. He's in the vault right now, and he said something about embezzlement and prison, sir."

"What! How dare he! The money's as good as there! I have stock certificates worth millions, and I can back up all our funds." He sneered at the cowering clerk. "Send the bank examiner in here immediately. He'll be facing slander charges if he keeps on as he has."

Hiram left quickly and brought the examiner to the office. "Mr. Bledsoe, this is Conrad Skundberg, from the territorial capital in Oklahoma City." The clerk darted out and closed the door behind him.

"What's this I hear about you bandying about my name and accusing me of embezzlement!" Bledsoe's deep brown eyes pierced the bank examiner's gaze. "Do you realize I can sue you for slander?"

"And do you realize, Mr. Bledsoe, that I can put you away for twenty years to life?" Skundberg countered.

"Look, this whole thing is preposterous! The funds are there.

I have enough stock certificates here to buy and sell this bank ten times over!"

"Those stock certificates—are they Henerow stock?"

"Why yes, they are. So you've heard already. Then you should know what I'm talking about."

"I'm not sure you do, Bledsoe. That stock isn't worth the parchment it's printed on!" He shook his bald head, his Adam's apple bobbing above his string tie. "If you've secured the funds of this bank with Henerow stock, you're a crook! And you'll rot in prison—if they don't hang you."

"Before we say things we'll both regret, how about joining me at the telegraph office? We can wire the bank in Oklahoma City and see if the Henerow account is good or not. After all, why would the *New York Times* lie?" Bledsoe reached for his copy of the *Times* but couldn't find it. "It's here somewhere— I just had it on my desk."

"Oh, really? And what did it say?"

Bledsoe rang for Hiram, who popped his head in the door almost immediately. "Yessir?"

"Abernathy, where's my *Times*?"

"I think I saw Mr. Greenleaf with it. Would you like me to find him and get it back?"

Bledsoe blanched. He said to the examiner, "Please wait right here. I'll be back in a moment." He headed for the door.

"I'm afraid I can't let you do that, Mr. Bledsoe."

"Then come with me to the telegrapher's. I have to check out something right now."

"All right. But make it snappy."

Bledsoe ran to the telegraph office, Skundberg on his heels. He handed Jeremiah a message to send. When the people at the other end replied, Bledsoe cried out in disbelief and ran from the office.

"Spike!" he yelled, "I need you!"

The man with one ear and two of his friends came at a trot. "What's up, Boss?"

"We have to leave here now. Don't let anyone stop us from getting out of here."

Conrad Skundberg followed Bledsoe from the telegrapher's and waved for the marshal. "Marshal, I want this man placed under arrest for embezzlement and grand larceny."

"Oh, you do?" Marshal Teddison ambled over. "Seems to me you're the one who should be arrested—for disturbing the peace." The marshal drew his six-shooter and aimed it at the bank examiner.

Spike drew his weapon, too, and leveled it at the bank examiner. "It's about time you left town, mister. You can do it on a horse or in a pine box—take your pick."

"On the other hand," came a steady voice from across the street, "you can all drop your weapons."

Everyone turned to see Ki standing next to Jessica Starbuck —Winchesters aimed squarely at Bledsoe, Spike and Teddison. Spike threw himself down behind a watering trough and fired at Ki. Teddison dropped back into the doorway and fired at Jessie. Spike's friends faded into the background to watch.

Ki and Jessie fired together, each hitting a target. The marshal dropped his weapon, his arm limp and bleeding. Spike fired again, this time with his left hand. Ki shot several times through the trough, but the bullets changed trajectory in the water. He crouched behind a barrel and peppered the trough.

"Give it up, Bledsoe," Jessie called. "We've got guns all up and down the street. You're completely covered and there's no way you can go."

Bledsoe looked, and Spike stopped shooting long enough to look. At both ends of the street, citizens of Harcourtville stood, rifles ready. Bert Harcourt fired several shots into the air.

"Come on, Bledsoe—let's go," Bert hollered. "You're about to be the guest of honor at a necktie party. I'd really rather cut you down where you stand, but I can't shoot an unarmed man."

The bank president grabbed the examiner as a shield and brought out a two-shot derringer. "All right, now I have the upper hand. I'm leaving, and I'm taking this guy with me. If anyone tries to stop me, I'll blow his brains all over the street!" He pushed the hostage ahead of him.

Conrad Skundberg had enough sense to stay perfectly still. He realized that a moving target might get shot. He refused to budge. He turned his head and said, "You kill me, and you've killed your shield."

Bledsoe held the man by the back of the collar and dragged him backward into the telegraph office. "If you won't move, I'll get another hostage!" he growled. He hit the bank examiner on the back of the neck and grabbed old Jeremiah as the unconscious man dropped.

"No, Mr. Bledsoe, not me," Jeremiah pleaded.

"Move, damn you!" Bledsoe nearly carried the frail old man out the front door, yelling, "Now I got me a hostage nobody wants to see dead. Everybody move back or Jeremiah gets it in the head."

Jessie called, "Jeremiah, don't move. Stand still."

The old man froze as Jessie drew a bead and let loose— hitting Bledsoe in the eye. He dropped to the sidewalk, his derringer still in his hand.

Bert Harcourt and Clarence Baumgartner and the rest of the town's men rushed Spike and Teddison and the others. Everyone concerned with Bledsoe or Teddison was rounded up and placed in jail until a new town marshal could be hired.

"Coffee's on me," Mike called out. "And pie till it runs out."

Bert took Jessie aside. "You were wonderful. I'm really going to miss you when you leave. That is, unless you'd care to stay."

Jessie hugged him and snuggled in his arm. "Let's talk about that later—in bed. Right now, I'd like some of Mom's gooseberry pie."

WESTERNS!

at least a savings of $3.00 each month below the publishers price. Second, there is never any shipping, handling or other hidden charges—Free home delivery. What's more there is no minimum number of books you must buy, you may return any selection for full credit and you can cancel your subscription at any time. A TRUE VALUE!

Mail the coupon below

To start your subscription and receive 2 FREE WESTERNS, fill out the coupon below and mail it today. We'll send your first shipment which includes 2 FREE BOOKS as soon as we receive it.

Mail To:
True Value Home Subscription Services, Inc.
P.O. Box 5235
120 Brighton Road
Clifton, New Jersey 07015-5235

10527-X

YES! I want to start receiving the very best Westerns being published today. Send me my first shipment of 6 Westerns for me to preview FREE for 10 days. If I decide to keep them, I'll pay for just 4 of the books at the low subscriber price of $2.45 each; a total of $9.80 (a $17.70 value). Then each month I'll receive the 6 newest and best Westerns to preview Free for 10 days. If I'm not satisfied I may return them within 10 days and owe nothing. Otherwise I'll be billed at the special low subscriber rate of $2.45 each; a total of $14.70 (at least a $17.70 value) and save $3.00 off the publishers price. There are never any shipping, handling or other hidden charges. I understand I am under no obligation to purchase any number of books and I can cancel my subscription at any time, no questions asked. In any case the 2 FREE books are mine to keep.

Name _____

Address _____ Apt. # _____

City _____ State _____ Zip _____

Telephone # _____

Signature _____

(if under 18 parent or guardian must sign)
Terms and prices subject to change.
Orders subject to acceptance by True Value Home Subscription Services, Inc.